#4
NOW WE'RE TALKING

Dean Hughes

Aladdin Paperbacks

First Aladdin Paperbacks edition May 1999

Copyright © 1999 by Dean Hughes

Aladdin Paperbacks
An imprint of Simon & Schuster
Children's Publishing Division
1230 Avenue of the Americas
New York, NY 10020

Also available in an Atheneum Books for Young Readers hardcover edition.

Designed by Ann Bobco

The text for this book was set in Caslon 540 Roman.

Printed and bound in the United States of America

10   9   8   7   6   5   4   3   2   1

The Library of Congress has cataloged the hardcover edition as follows:
Hughes, Dean, 1943–
Now we're talking / by Dean Hughes.
p.   cm.—(Scrappers #4)
Summary: Seventh grader Ollie loses his self-confidence as a pitcher when his weird habit of talking to himself on the mound signals his pitches to the batters and draws the anger of some of his teammates.
ISBN 0-689-81927-7 (hc).—ISBN 0-689-81937-4 (pbk)
[1. Baseball—Fiction. 2. Self-confidence—Fiction.] I. Title. II. Series: Hughes, Dean, 1943–   Scrappers ; #4.
PZ7.H87312Np   1999
[Fic]—dc21   98-44733

CHAPTER ONE

Ollie Allman hunched forward and stared at his catcher, Wilson Love. Wilson made a fist, hid it against his leg, and then pointed down with one finger. "Fastball," Ollie whispered. "Okay, relax," he told himself—out loud. "Wilson's mitt is a magnet. Release the ball and the mitt will pull it in."

He wound up and *fired* a pitch over the plate. The batter took a good cut, but late, and fouled the ball off.

Ollie took a deep breath. "Good pitch, Ollie," he said. And then he responded to his own words. "Thanks. But the mitt did it."

The batter was a kid named Eric Fellows, who was an all-around great athlete. Everyone in Wasatch City knew him. The guy could hit, but he also had the wheels to get to first base *quick*.

Ollie looked for the sign. One finger again. "That's right," he said. "More heat. Just use the magnet, Ollie my boy."

Ollie tossed a hard pitch, just off the plate, outside. Eric chased it and rolled a grounder toward first base.

Adam Pfitzer, the Scrappers' first baseman, charged the ball, scooped it up, and tagged the runner.

One away.

"Nice job, Adam!" Ollie called to his friend.

Adam grinned. "I almost forgot to go after the ball," he said. "I was thinking about something else."

Adam was almost always "thinking about something else."

Wanda Coates, the assistant coach, was yelling from the dugout, "Way to go, Ollie. Mow 'em down." She was a tall woman with reddish hair, and like her son, Thurlow, she looked like an athlete.

Ollie was nervous. The Scrappers had been up and down all season. But they had won a big game over the Stingrays the week before. Now they had to keep it going.

The truth was, Ollie didn't like being a pitcher. Too many things upset him—and then he couldn't throw strikes. So he looked for ways to control his thoughts. "When I use the magnet," he told himself, "no one can hit my pitches."

Ollie was *very* tall for a seventh-grader, and he had no flesh on his bones—like a six-foot skeleton. Kids had been teasing him for years about the way he talked to himself. But it was easier for him to know what he was thinking when he explained things to himself—and listened.

"Okay, Ollie," he said, "let the glove do the work."

The next batter—a boy named Kiesel—locked his eyes on Ollie. He looked serious. "Don't pay any attention to him," Ollie said. "Just look at Wilson."

Wilson signaled for a fastball again.

"Let's go, Ollie. Fire away," Gloria Gibbs was yelling. Her encouragement always sounded more like a threat. The girl made Ollie nervous.

"Fastball," Ollie said, a little too loudly. He

lowered his voice and added, "Just release the ball to the magnet." He blasted a fastball over the plate. Kiesel swung hard, but he got a little under the ball. It drifted toward center field, and it looked like an easy out.

As Jeremy Lim ran forward, he shielded his eyes with his glove. Then he shook his head, and it was clear he had lost the ball in the sun. He finally picked up on it again and charged forward, but the ball hit in front of him and skipped on by.

While Thurlow chased the ball down, Kiesel kept going and cruised all the way around to third.

The Hot Rod players were a bunch of loudmouths. They all started giving Jeremy a hard time. "Hey, kid, the ball is round, and it has stitches on it," one of them yelled. "You'll know it when you see it."

"They think they're so great," Ollie said. "They don't know about the magnet." But Ollie's confidence was shaken. That last pitch had come up higher than it was supposed to. Maybe the magnet hadn't worked.

Ollie's next two pitches also sailed high.

"Don't do this, Ollie," Ollie told himself. "The magnet will work if you concentrate on it."

But this time he let up a little—to make sure he threw a strike—and the pitch was *fat*. The batter, a guy named Rohrbach, slammed the ball hard on the ground toward Robbie Marquez, at third.

Robbie belly-flopped and knocked the ball down. Then he scrambled to his feet and made a pretty good throw. But it hit in the dirt in front of Adam. With a better stretch, Adam might have dug it out, but he tried to short-hop the ball, and it glanced off his glove. Kiesel scored from third, and Rohrbach kept right on rolling. He ended up at second.

As Kiesel ran to the dugout, some of the Hot Rods came out and gave him high fives.

"You've got no arm, Robbie," Rohrbach yelled.

Gloria walked over to Rohrbach and stuck a finger straight at his nose. "Shut up!" she said. "If you hit the ball to this side again, *I'll* go get it. And I just might throw it at *you*."

"Oooh, I'm scared," Rohrbach said. But

he did sound a little frightened. Gloria was not as big as he was, but she was solid, and she had a voice like gravel in a cement mixer.

The next batter was a moose of a guy named Meyers. Ollie told himself, "Forget the batters. Just see the glove." But he unleashed a floater, and Meyers hit the ball out of sight.

Trent Lubak, the Scrappers' left fielder, ran back to the fence, looked up, and watched the ball sail high over his head for a home run.

Ollie took a quick glance at big Meyers as he loped around the bases, and then he looked away. He stared off at Mount Timpanogos and tried to relax, but his insides were in an uproar. He needed something new to concentrate on. "This pitching rubber has power in it—from the center of the earth," he said. "It can help me more than any stupid magnetic glove."

"That's right, Ollie. You better talk to yourself about that one," one of the Hot Rods was yelling.

Gloria told the guy to shut up, but then she walked to Ollie and said, in a voice that cut like a dull knife, "What's going on, Ollie?" She was chomping on a big wad of gum.

Ollie knew this was her idea of coming over to settle him down. But she sounded more like she was accusing him.

Tracy Matlock, the Scrappers' second baseman, came trotting over. "He's doing all right, Gloria," she said. "Stay off his back."

"All I asked him was—"

"Just leave him alone and let him pitch."

"Hey, kids, that's enough." The coach was walking toward the mound. He stopped in front of Ollie and folded his arms over his chest. "Ollie, you're doing fine. We can get those runs back. Just relax and throw."

What was bothering Ollie, even more than the game, was his teammates and his coach all looking so worried—no matter what they said. Gloria had worked hard lately not to yell at her own teammates. But every time Ollie made a bad pitch, he felt like she was having to bite her tongue not to say anything.

Ollie tried not to think about any of this now. He kept his foot on the pitching rubber. He was almost sure he felt power seeping into his foot, rising up through his body and into his arm. This was going to work.

And once everyone left him alone, he threw a

good pitch to the next batter—at the knees and on the inside part of the plate. The batter went down after it, and he slapped it toward second. Tracy took a step to her left and made a good stop. But as she tried to dig the ball out of her glove, she dropped it.

She chased after the ball, reached for it, and accidentally kicked it. By the time she got to it again, the runner had crossed first base.

"Tracy, what's that—your clown act?" Gloria screamed.

Tracy tossed the ball to Ollie, and then she said, "Gloria, shut your big mouth."

"You didn't have to hurry," Adam was saying. "You had plenty of time."

"Hey, we're all right," Coach Carlton called out. "Don't start chewing on each other."

Ollie felt like he needed earplugs. It was bad enough that his team was making so many errors. What he didn't need was all this fussing among them. "Just listen to *me*," he told himself. "Forget everyone else. The power from the pitching rubber can't be stopped."

But Ollie was rattled. He walked the next batter on four pitches.

And the noise got worse. People in the bleachers were shouting, and the Hot Rods were keeping up a steady stream of insults. Ollie was glad his mom and dad hadn't been able to make it to the game. That would only have made him more nervous.

With two runners on and only one out, Ollie knew he had to do something before this game was out of reach.

The next batter was a guy from Ollie's church group, David Dietz. He wasn't much of an athlete. "Okay, Ollie, your power is coming from the earth," Ollie told himself. But he didn't believe that one now. He tried to think of something else, but he could hardly hear himself talk over the noise from the bleachers and the field.

Ollie tossed a pitch over the plate without much on it. Dietz lashed at it and missed.

"Okay. Now you can get him." But his next pitch was about the same, and this time Dietz timed it. He drove a line drive to the left side.

It looked like a sure base hit, but Gloria leaped high and snagged the ball in the webbing of her glove. The runner on second had broken toward third and Gloria turned to double him up.

But she had to wait. Tracy was late running to the bag. By the time she got there, the runner had made it back to second.

"Come on, Tracy. Where were you?" Gloria shouted. "We could have been out of the inning." Then she yelled at Ollie, "You're lucky I can jump. Start *throwing*, will you?"

Gloria's words were like rocks. Ollie tried to let them bounce off, but they hit hard. He stepped back on the rubber with doubts in his mind. He tried to think of something to tell himself. "Ollie, your arm is a slingshot. Just let the ball fly." But he didn't believe that one either.

He threw a pitch so high that Wilson had to jump for it. And then all the yelling started again—from the Hot Rods, from the crowd, and worst of all, from Gloria, his own teammate.

Gloria's father had a voice like his daughter's, and he was bellowing over the noise of the crowd, "Hey, coach, pull that kid. Put a pitcher out there."

Ollie aimed his next pitch and got it in the strike zone. But it had nothing on it, and the batter *slammed* it.

Ollie looked at the ground, not at the fence in right field—over which he figured the ball would soon disappear. But then he heard a cheer, and he looked around.

Thurlow had made a long run and had snagged the ball.

The Scrappers were out of the top of the first inning. Ollie let out his breath. He was mostly just relieved—not really satisfied with the job he had done.

He was glad only three runs had scored, but he hated to think what might happen next inning. So he walked to Mr. Carlton. "Coach," he said, "you better let Adam pitch."

"You'll be fine," Coach Carlton told him.

"But I don't have any control today."

"Ollie," Coach Carlton said, putting his hand on Ollie's shoulder, "in one sense, this game doesn't matter that much. We have no chance to win the first-half championship. The important thing is for you to work through a tough time like this—so that you'll be mentally ready in the second half. You're a good pitcher, but you're trying too hard. You need to relax."

Ollie walked back to the dugout with the coach. On the bench, Gloria was still chewing gum and still chewing out Tracy. Then, before she noticed Ollie, she said, "We've just *got* to find someone who can pitch. I think we should go with Thurlow. He looked good in that last game."

When she looked up and saw the coach—and Ollie—she flinched and then ducked her head again.

Coach Carlton spoke softly but firmly. "I'm not going to put up with any more of that kind of stuff, Gloria. I've been talking to you about this all season. You do a little better for a game or two, and then you start all over again."

"Okay. Okay," Gloria said. She leaned back and looked away. But she didn't apologize to Ollie.

Ollie walked into the fenced-in area that served as a dugout. The place was silent. Ollie figured the players were all telling themselves,

"If I can't say anything good, I won't say anything at all." And there was nothing good to say about him right now. That much he knew for sure.

CHAPTER TWO

Coach Carlton and Wanda Coates walked out to their coaches' boxes. The Scrappers sat on the bench like a row of statues.

Ollie concentrated on Jeremy. He had a theory that if he looked really hard at people, he could send positive forces, like radio waves, into their brains. "Get a hit," he whispered, and he squinted hard to push the thought through the air.

Ollie didn't really believe stuff like that would work. It was just something he fooled around with in his mind. But he did spend a lot of time thinking—and talking to himself—even though he knew it made other kids think he was weird.

"Get a hit, Jeremy," Gloria screamed. "Do *something* right today." That seemed to be her idea of "encouraging."

Jeremy took a hard cut at the first pitch—even though it was level with his chin—and missed. Rohrbach was the pitcher, and he could really hum the ball.

"Hey, what are you swinging at?" Gloria yelled. "That pitch was over your head."

Adam was sitting next to Ollie. The two had become pretty good friends lately. Ollie whispered to Adam, "What's her problem? She acts like *she* never does anything wrong."

"That's how Gloria has always been," Adam said. "Her whole family is the same way. My dad and I went out to their scrap yard one time, and ol' Jack Gibbs talked to my dad like he was some kind of idiot."

Jeremy took a swing at another high pitch and missed again. Gloria moaned.

Adam said, "I thought we were getting along all right after that swimming party last week. But as soon as we start playing bad, all the players start blaming each other."

"Most of them are blaming me," Ollie said. "Every time I walk someone, I feel like the whole team hates me."

"Hey, I feel the same way when I'm pitching."

Jeremy reached up and poked the next pitch. The ball looped toward right field, but the second baseman ran a few steps back and hauled it in. One away.

"What was he swinging at?" Gloria mumbled as she walked to the on-deck circle, but at least she didn't yell at Jeremy.

Wilson was doing that. "Jeremy, you swung at three balls!"

Robbie stepped into the batter's box. He took a couple of balls, outside, and then he got his pitch and met it head-on. The ball jumped off his bat and shot straight up the middle for a base hit.

Robbie hustled to first, rounded the base, and then held on.

"We're on our way now," Wanda yelled from her first base coach's box.

Gloria took a strike—and argued with the umpire about it—but then *stung* the next pitch hard past the shortstop.

Robbie rounded second and seemed headed for third. But suddenly he threw on the brakes. The coach was holding up his arms: the signal to stop at second. For a moment, Ollie thought that was no problem. But then he realized that Gloria was also on her way to second, running fast.

Robbie and Gloria saw each other at about the same time—both of them nearing the base. And both stopped.

At that point, Robbie should have kept going back to second. Gloria might have made it back to first. Instead, Robbie spun and took off for third. But he didn't have a chance. The throw was on the money, and the third baseman put the tag on him.

Robbie had made a mistake. But it was Gloria who had created the mess in the first place, by not watching the coach and seeing that he had the stop sign on.

Of course, that wasn't how Gloria saw it. "Why did you stop, Robbie?" she shouted. "You were halfway to third."

Coach Carlton yelled, "Time-out, ump," and he ran onto the field, straight toward Gloria. When he got to her, he did all the talking, and Gloria did a lot of nodding.

"It's the same old thing," Adam said. "She'll shut up for a while, and then she starts jawing at everyone again."

"Even if she doesn't yell at me, I know what she's thinking," Ollie said.

When the coach walked away from Gloria, she stood with her hands on her hips and her mouth clamped shut. But her face was flaming red. She looked ready to eat second base.

When Thurlow stepped up to the plate—batting cleanup today for the first time—he stood in the box with his bat hanging down. He didn't look ready. But he liked the first pitch, and his arms—his quick wrists—came to life. He connected, and the ball blasted off on a long arc and disappeared over the left field fence.

Ollie jumped to his feet. "How did he do that?" he asked himself, out loud. The score was suddenly 3 to 2, and the Scrappers were back in the game.

Wilson was up after that, but he had trouble with Rohrbach's fastball. He did connect pretty well on one pitch, but he swung late, and he fouled the ball off. In the end, he struck out, and the inning was over.

Ollie felt a little better when he walked back to the mound. He took his practice pitches, then placed his foot on the rubber and stared at Wilson's mitt.

Ollie could throw a decent change-up, and once in a while he tried a curveball, but his fastball was his best pitch. And that's what Wilson called for.

"Fastball," Ollie said out loud, and then, as Wilson set up the target, he added, "Low and away. My eyes are laser beams. They'll guide the ball to anything I look at."

Ollie got the ball a little too far outside, however, and the batter, a guy named Ricky Tobias, didn't swing.

"Ollie, focus your laser on the target," Ollie said. "Lock on before you throw this time."

Wilson called for another fastball and set the target on the inside of the plate. "That's right," Ollie said. "Keep the ball moving in and out. The laser is now *locked*."

But Tobias seemed to know what was coming. He stepped back and jerked the ball to left field, just inside the foul line. The ball got past Trent and rolled all the way to the fence.

Tobias ended up with a double.

That's how it seemed to go for a while, too.

The batters were timing Ollie perfectly. He tried his change-up and his curve, but the Hot Rods were hitting everything he threw.

Gloria wasn't saying a word. In fact, the whole team was silent. But Ollie knew what the players were thinking. When Rohrbach pasted the ball hard over Tracy's head and drove in two runs, Wilson stepped out from behind the plate. "What are you doing out there, Ollie?" he yelled. "Don't try to aim your pitches."

"Yeah, right," Ollie mumbled to himself. He turned around and looked toward the mountains. "But if I start walking people, then what's he going to say?"

The Hot Rods ended up with three runs in the inning, and now they were ahead 6 to 2. The Scrappers were deep in a hole again.

The batters didn't come through in the bottom of the second either. And Ollie didn't help matters. With runners on first and second, he struck out.

When he walked back to the dugout, no one would even look at him. He sat down on the bench next to Adam. "I tried," he said.

"I know."

"Then how come everyone's mad at me?"

"They're not. They're just mad we're playing so bad."

But Ollie didn't believe that. He was sure the players thought he was the problem.

In the third, Angela Hobart led off for the Hot Rods. She hit a hard grounder right at Tracy. The ball took a low hop and scooted under her glove. Thurlow probably could have held the hit to a single, but he took it easy as he loped toward the ball.

Hobart saw that and took off for second. Once Thurlow saw what was happening, he threw hard to second, and Gloria made a good catch, but her tag was too late.

Gloria came away from the play steaming. She kicked the bag so hard she was lucky she didn't hurt her foot. But she didn't say anything to Thurlow. She walked back to her position.

Ollie looked out at Thurlow, who was looking down at the ground. Maybe he was disgusted with himself, or maybe he was mad at Gloria. There was no way to tell.

Wanda yelled, "Thurlow, come on. That's no way to play this game."

Ollie saw Thurlow stiffen. Then he turned and walked back to his position.

Of course, the Hot Rods loved this. "Thurlow, that's no way to play this game," they yelled, imitating Wanda. And some were shouting, "Hey, Ollie, thanks for the help. You're the best player on *our* team."

All this was driving Ollie nuts. "Settle down," he told himself. "Don't let them bother you. Lock in your laser."

Wilson signaled for a curve. "Good idea," Ollie said. "Let's go with the curve. The laser can bend."

Ollie threw a good curve, but Dietz laid off the pitch and took the called strike.

"That's all right. Now fire a fastball right on by him." He watched for Wilson to set up. "Keep it down," Ollie whispered.

Dietz timed the pitch just right and stroked a line drive toward Adam at first. Adam reacted late, and the ball whizzed past him into right field.

This time Thurlow ran harder. He picked up the ball smoothly and threw to the plate. Hobart had thought about coming home, but the throw reached Wilson on the fly, and she held up and retreated to third. The only trouble was, Thurlow had overthrown the cutoff. Dietz saw that and took off for second.

Wilson fired to second, but he hurried himself and threw high. The ball sailed into center, and now Hobart came home to score. At the same time, Dietz got up and ran for third.

Jeremy hustled and got the ball, but instead of throwing home, he threw to third—where he had no chance of making a play. Dietz saw the throw and darted toward the plate.

Robbie took Jeremy's throw and spun toward home. But it was too late. Dietz was crossing the plate.

When all the dust settled, two more runs had scored. "What a bunch of idiots!" Rohrbach yelled.

Gloria was sputtering and looking around at her teammates. Finally, she couldn't hold it in. "Don't any of you *birdbrains* know what you're doing?" she screamed. "What's going on around here?"

Ollie put his hands on his hips and looked at the sky. The score was 8 to 2, and still no one was out.

And now Coach Carlton was walking toward him—probably to pull him off the mound. That was fine with Ollie.

Instead, the coach waved the infielders over. Once everyone had gathered around the mound, Coach Carlton said, calmly, "Kids, you're forgetting what we've worked on all these weeks. You all need to calm down and *think*."

"Everyone's throwing the ball around like a bunch of T-ball players," Gloria said. "No one seems to—"

"*Quiet!*" the coach demanded. "Gloria, you apparently don't believe me. This is your final warning. You make one more negative statement to your teammates and I'm taking you out of the game."

Gloria ducked her head.

"All right," Coach Carlton said. "We're okay. Ollie, you're pitching fine, but I think the batters can hear what you're saying to yourself. You may be giving your pitches away."

"I can hear him half the time," Wilson said. "I know darn well the batters can, too."

"Okay," Ollie said. But that worried him— and sort of made him mad. What gave batters the right to listen in on his private conversations?

Still, Ollie tried to keep his voice down after that. And things did go better. He whiffed Richie Thatcher, the second baseman, on a change-up. Then he got the next two batters on ground balls. Gloria made a great play on a ball hit to her right to get the final out.

Ollie was just glad to get back to the bench. What he wanted more than anything was for the game to be over—or for someone else to pitch.

Right now, everyone was knotted up in groups of two or three, talking, taking sides. The coach had worked all season to bring the players together, and now everything was falling apart.

But Jeremy didn't seem to let that bother him. He punched out a nice single, and then Robbie drilled a pitch into center for a double. Jeremy had had to wait to see whether the ball would get past the outfielders, so he didn't score, but runners were on second and third when Gloria came up.

Rohrbach must have been shaken. He walked Gloria on four pitches.

So Thurlow was up. Once again, he stood at

the plate like he didn't care. The first pitch was high, and he let it go by. But the next pitch was over the plate, and his quick hands sprung into action. He *swatted* the ball, and it sailed high and long—over the center field fence.

Way over the fence. Grand slam!

For a moment, the players seemed to forget all their bad feelings. They emptied the bench and ran out to greet their scoring teammates.

The Scrappers were back in the game. The score was 8 to 6.

CHAPTER THREE

Ollie had a new chance. If he could hold these guys for a couple of innings, his team could come back. Maybe all the Scrappers had to do was get Thurlow up to bat with runners on base one more time.

But Ollie wasn't comfortable. He was trying to talk softly, so the batters couldn't hear him, and he really missed the sound of his own voice. "The laser works. Trust the laser," he mumbled under his breath. And then he added, "Keep the ball on the outside of the plate."

He came with his hard stuff—a little outside. It was a good pitch, but Kiesel reached for the ball and plunked a looper into right field for a single.

Wilson ran out to the mound when the play was over. "Hey, Ollie, I heard you say, 'Keep the ball on the outside of the plate.' The batter knew what to look for."

"You heard me say that?"

"I sure did."

"I thought I whispered."

"No way. I heard you, clear as anything. I've even heard some of those kids saying, 'Just listen. He'll tell you what he's going to throw.'"

So Ollie kept his mouth shut when Rohrbach stepped up to the plate. He tried to get some real steam on his fastball—and only *think* about the laser—but the pitch got away from him and once again sailed high.

Ollie made sure the next pitch was a strike, but he took too much off it. Rohrbach hit a screamer into center field.

Jeremy charged the ball, took it on the first bounce, and threw to the cutoff. The runners held up at first and second.

Ollie couldn't believe what was happening. Nothing was working right now. His motion felt terrible. Why wouldn't the coach just let Adam pitch?

Gloria yelled, "Don't worry, Ollie. Make a good pitch, and we'll back you up." At least she was saying the right things. But she still sounded mad.

Ollie tried to think what to do, but when he couldn't speak, the words in his head didn't seem real. And his mind games weren't working. Meyers was up to bat. If he banged out another homer, the Scrappers would be buried again.

Wilson signaled for a curve, and Ollie thought that was smart. Meyers was aggressive and would probably be swinging free. Ollie tried to snap off a good curve. But the pitch hung high in the strike zone.

Meyers was off balance, but he got decent wood on the ball and lifted it out to left field. Trent jogged into position, caught it, and made a strong throw to third to hold the runners.

Robbie waited for the throw, but at the last second he must have glanced to see whether the runner on second had tagged up. He reached out to make the catch, but the ball bounced off his glove and rolled toward the bat rack. By the time he chased it down, the runners were standing on second and third.

Gloria turned her back and strolled toward the outfield. She stopped on the edge of the grass, and Ollie was sure she was doing some talking of her own. In a way, it was worse than if she just blew up. Ollie knew that the whole team could feel her anger.

"Come on, Gloria, let's play," Tracy called to her.

Gloria shook her head, said nothing, and returned to her position.

The next batter was a new player in the game, a little guy, who didn't look like he could hurt the Scrappers much.

He took a couple of pitches, high, and Ollie knew he was hoping for a walk. But Ollie didn't want to give the little kid a free ride. He also didn't want to load up the bases.

Ollie told himself, "Just ease off and throw a strike. He can't hit it." He threw an easy pitch, and the kid swung hard. The ball arced into center field, and Ollie could see that it would be an easy catch.

But Jeremy had seen that hard swing and misjudged how solidly the ball was hit. He ran back a few steps, and then he reversed himself and charged forward. The ball bounced in front of him, and he caught it on one hop.

The runners had to hold up halfway to see whether Jeremy would catch the ball. Only one run scored, but now runners were on first and third, and there was still only one out.

Ollie knew what Gloria was thinking. Jeremy's mistake was the same one he had made several times earlier in the season. Why was he suddenly messing up the same way again?

But Ollie took a hard look at Gloria, and she didn't say a word. She was working her chaw of bubble gum hard, her jaw pumping like a heart muscle. She spit into her glove.

When Ollie turned around, he saw Wilson running to the mound. "That little kid heard what you said on that last pitch. He knew you were easing off, and he was ready."

"What do you mean? I didn't say it. I just thought it."

"Then I can read your mind—because I heard it."

Ollie couldn't believe this. There seemed to be a window in his forehead. People could look right inside and see all his thoughts. What was he supposed to do?

"Clench your teeth, Ollie. Don't let yourself talk."

"Okay, okay."

Wilson ran back to the plate. But Ollie felt as though he were about to go nuts. The coach wouldn't take him out of the game, and all the players were down on him. He could feel it.

The next batter—another sub—dug in, and then said, "Okay, Ollie, tell me what you're going to do."

Ollie knew he couldn't say a word this time.

So he took the sign—fastball—and saw that Wilson was setting up low. He tried to imagine his pitch but not talk about it. He wanted to believe in the magnet, or in the laser beam, but none of that was working for him. He just had to throw the ball.

He felt awkward as he wound up and almost weak as he threw. The batter swiped at the ball and drove it hard toward third base.

The ball got to Robbie on one hop. It was a perfect double-play ball.

Robbie turned, set his feet, gave Tracy a moment to get to the bag, and then shot the ball to second.

Tracy took the throw and dragged her foot across the bag, just the way she had been taught. But as she was turning, she hurried her throw to first. The ball hit the dirt in front of Adam and bounced over his glove.

Another run scored. And another runner took a free base and moved into scoring position.

Ollie looked over at Gloria and saw that she had given up. She was standing with her shoulders slumped. She didn't even look mad. He glanced around the field and noticed that everyone else looked the same way.

Coach Carlton was clapping his hands and saying, "Hang in there, Ollie. We're all right." But he didn't seem to mean it. The Scrappers had come a long way this season, but right now they seemed worse off than ever. No one could do much of anything right.

Ollie stepped back on the rubber, but he had given up, too. He looked at Wilson, who signaled for a fastball. But suddenly Ollie didn't feel strong enough to throw one.

He stepped off the rubber and turned around. He tried to think of something he could tell himself, but when he looked toward the outfield, he saw Jeremy standing with his arms crossed over his chest. The kid was obviously expecting more of the same.

Ollie yelled, "Time-out." He walked off the mound and marched straight to the third base coach's box. "I can't do it," he told Coach Carlton.

"Ollie, you need to work through this," the coach said. "You can—"

"No, I can't. Take me out of the game. Please."

"Okay. But, Ollie, you're a good pitcher. The team needs you." He put his hand on Ollie's shoulder. "We'll work on some things at practice, and you'll be—"

"No. I don't want to pitch. I don't even want to play. All I do is let everybody down all the time."

"Ollie, that's not true."

But Ollie wasn't listening. He stepped past the coach and then tramped off toward the dugout. Every step was an effort, he felt so powerless. But he wanted to get to the dugout, sit down, and let the game go on. Maybe then, everyone would stop looking at him.

Ollie heard the coach yell to Adam to take the mound, and he called for Chad Corrigan to go out and play first base.

When Ollie reached the dugout, Cindy Jones said, "Don't feel bad, Ollie. You did okay."

Ollie walked to the end of the dugout and sat down. He tried to think of something to tell himself, but it suddenly hit him how weird that was. He was a weird kid, that's all. The other players didn't talk to themselves. No one did.

So he pressed his lips together, hard as he could.

Adam was warming up and looking good. Ollie figured that from now on Adam and Thurlow could be the pitchers. Ollie would play first base or just sit on the bench. And if the coach tried to force him to pitch, he would quit the team. He just couldn't go through another game like this.

But Adam didn't do a whole lot better than Ollie. By the time the Hot Rods took the field, the score was 12 to 6.

When the Scrappers walked back to the dugout, no one had much of anything to say. Adam sat down next to Ollie, but all he said was, "We stink."

And that turned out to be about right. The Scrappers went down, one-two-three, and then trudged back to the field. Adam walked the first two batters, and then the Hot Rods started smashing the ball again. Before they made an out, the Hot Rods scored four runs, and the game was over. According to the league's rule, if a team got ahead by ten after the third inning, it automatically got the victory.

The Hot Rods rubbed it in plenty, too. They lined up and slapped hands with the Scrappers, but they were mouthing off the whole time. As Ollie went through the line, about half the players thanked him for announcing his pitches before he threw them.

Ollie didn't say a word, but he felt stupid. And when the coach gave the players his usual pep talk, Ollie couldn't believe what the man had to say. "Look, kids, it was just a bad day. We sort of came apart out there, but we played well last week, and we can do it again."

Gloria raised her hand.

"Yes?" Coach Carlton said.

"Look, I'm not yelling at anyone, and this is nothing against Ollie and Adam, but don't we need to try some other players on the mound?

I've pitched before, and Thurlow has. Wilson has a good arm, too. We'll never win if we can't get better pitching."

The coach took a long breath. Ollie could see that he was irritated. "Gloria, our defense was terrible today. We made too many mental errors. We have two very good pitchers, but we have to back them up. And I don't mean just back them up with our gloves. We have to back them up with our attitudes, too."

But Ollie said, "Coach, she's right about me. I can't pitch. I told you before, I don't want to do it anymore."

"Ollie," Coach Carlton said, "I don't want to hear any more of that. You've got a great arm. You didn't have a good day today, but for us to have any chance at the second-half championship, we've got to have you on the mound."

Ollie looked down at the grass. He wasn't going to tell the coach in front of all the players, but he was quitting the team. He just couldn't stand the thought of pitching again.

CHAPTER FOUR

Ollie was sitting in his family room when his mother got home that afternoon. The family's mutt—half Labrador, half everything else—was cuddled up next to him on the couch. Ollie was rubbing the young dog's neck and head, hardly aware that he was doing it.

Ollie had tried talking things out with himself for a while, but he kept coming back to the same dead end. He had to quit the team.

Ollie could tell that his mom sensed something was wrong. She sat down next to him and asked what was going on. Ollie told her the whole story.

"So you're going to quit?" Mrs. Allman said.

"Yep."

"But you love baseball. That's all you've talked about since the season started."

"I know. I'll just watch it from now on. I can't pitch, and the coach keeps telling me that's what he wants me to do."

"So what are you going to do all summer?"

"Sit here with Winnie the Poop Dog. Maybe eat some Popsicles."

His mother laughed, but Ollie knew she understood how disappointed he was. She and Ollie were a lot alike. Both were tall and lean, and both looked within themselves for answers. Ollie didn't expect his mother to solve this problem now.

"What are you *really* going to do?" His mom had her briefcase on her lap, but now she set it on the floor and reached her arm around Ollie's shoulders.

"There's nothing I can do. I already told the coach I didn't want to pitch, but he won't listen to me."

"Maybe he's right. Maybe you need to work through this and not give up on yourself."

"Yeah, right. And maybe we can teach Winnie not to poop on the back porch."

His mom laughed again. "Well, I'm still trying to teach her," she said. "If I won't give up on her, why should I give up on you?"

"Hey, what are you talking about? I don't poop on the back porch."

When his mom laughed hard, she wrinkled up her nose, and her gums showed. She was pretty—except when she did that. "No," she said, "I meant maybe you could practice with the coach—try to see what you've been doing wrong."

"It won't do any good. He's already worked with me a lot. But once I get in a game, everything changes." Ollie slumped down and stretched his bare legs out. They reached halfway across the family room. Winnie nestled closer, and Ollie rubbed her behind the ear.

"Maybe so, Ollie. But I don't think you really want to quit. You could have stayed around and told the coach after the game—or called him on the phone. I think you're still trying to figure out a way to keep playing."

"Not really."

"Yes. Really."

Ollie rolled his head sideways and looked up at his mother. "Mom," he said, "do you think I'm weird?"

"You're *interesting*. That's what you are."

"You're the only person who thinks so."

"Ollie, I like you the way you are—and I've never been wrong in my whole life. Not once."

"What about that time you—"

"Shut up, weird boy."

They both laughed, but then his mom said, "Okay, so you're a little . . . different."

"That's just a nice way to say 'weird.'"

"Everyone is weird, Ollie. Every single person is different from everyone else. And we all have our own odd little ways of doing things. But that's good, not bad. Who wants to be the same as a million other people?"

"Come on, Mom. Some things are normal weird, but talking to yourself—the way I do—is weird weird."

His mother reached out and took hold of his hand. "Ollie, you've always done that. You don't have any brothers or sisters, so you've spent a lot of time alone. What's more natural than that—to talk out loud when you're playing by yourself?"

"Mom, I'm not a little kid anymore."

"I know. But I'm just trying to help you understand. We've moved so many times over the years, and it hasn't always been easy for you to find new friends. Your dad and I both work long hours, too. So you spend a lot more time by yourself than most kids. I don't think it's strange at all that you talk to yourself. I do that myself sometimes. I'll be sitting at my desk, trying to sort out my thoughts, and I'll just start—"

"That's not the same. I talk so loud that I tell the other team what pitches I'm throwing. The players on my own team are mad at me about that."

"But if you quit playing, you'll *really* be letting the team down. Do you really want to do that?"

That's all Ollie needed: another reason to feel guilty. "You're not helping me, Mom. You're just getting me all mixed up again."

"Well, good. I think you need to think a lot more about all this before you give up on yourself—and on your team."

With that she got up and walked to her bedroom.

Ollie was left alone with Winnie. "What are we going to do, Poop Dog?" he said. "Mom's not going to let either one of us off the hook."

Ollie answered for Winnie. "I guess we both need to learn to control our pitches."

Then Ollie spoke for himself. "You probably will, sooner or later, Pooper, but I doubt I will."

Mrs. Allman had told Ollie to keep thinking, but he didn't. He spent the evening playing computer games and watching TV, trying not to think at all. He told himself he would make a decision in the morning—and then call the coach. But the next morning, after his parents had gone to work, he was still putting the whole thing off.

Then Adam showed up. He yelled for Ollie instead of ringing the doorbell, and then he stood on the porch looking confused—like he couldn't remember why he was there. He was wearing shorts, and his legs looked as long and white as birch trees.

"We don't have practice this morning, do we?" Ollie asked him.

"No. I just came over to see how you're doing. Are you feeling okay?"

"No."

"Hey, I messed up just as much as you did."

"So do you feel okay?"

Adam seemed surprised by the question—or maybe by his answer. "No. Not really," he said.

"I think I'm going to quit the team," Ollie said. "Do you want a Popsicle?"

"Sure."

Ollie motioned him inside, and they walked into the kitchen. Ollie got a box out of the freezer compartment of the refrigerator. "Orange, grape, or banana?" he asked.

"Why do you want to quit?"

"Do you like banana?"

"Sure."

"Good. I don't." He handed one to Adam. "Because I stink. And I'm getting worse, not better."

"Those guys on the Hot Rods knew what you were throwing. That's why they were hitting your pitches. All you have to do is keep your mouth shut, and you'll be all right."

"I *can't* keep my mouth shut. That's the problem."

Adam sat down. He hit his Popsicle against the edge of the kitchen table to break the halves apart. Then he bit at the plastic wrapper to start a rip in it. "Why do you have to talk to yourself?" he asked.

"Because I'm 'weird boy.'"

"Hey, I'm the weird guy around here. Everyone says that."

"Who does?"

"How long have you lived in Wasatch? Kids have been telling me I'm strange all my life."

"Why?"

"Because . . . I don't know . . . instead of thinking about what I'm doing, I think about other stuff. And the stuff I'm doing gets all fouled up with what I'm thinking."

Ollie knew what Adam meant. He had seen him forget he was playing baseball while he was standing at first base. "It's sort of the same thing with me," Ollie said. "I can't concentrate unless I can hear myself say what I'm thinking."

Adam had the banana Popsicle in his mouth. He looked at Ollie curiously, as though he hadn't quite understood.

"My mom says I'm weird because we move too much, and I don't have any brothers and sisters."

Adam pulled the Popsicle out of his mouth. "How come you move so much?"

Ollie sat down across from him at the table.

"My dad is just too good at what he does. He manages transmission shops. Every time his company has one that isn't making money, the boss sends him there to get things going right."

"Can he always figure out what to do?"

"Yep. Every time. But that means we've moved four times in the last five years. I end up playing on a different team almost every year."

"Did you talk to yourself in those other places?"

Ollie had to think about that. "Not as much. But I usually wasn't a pitcher. And I didn't get so nervous."

"Look, you can pitch at practice—right?"

"Yeah."

"Then why do you have trouble in the games?"

"Because everybody makes so much noise."

"Maybe you need some earplugs."

"It's not *only* the noise. I can look at everybody and tell what they're thinking. They don't *expect* me to throw good pitches."

"And who gets the players thinking that way?"

"Me, I guess."

"No, Ollie. It's mostly Gloria. She's so negative all the time that she gets everybody else down on you. And me. It's the same when I pitch."

"So what can we do about it?"

"Well, I've been thinking about that, and I've got an idea. Come with me. Bring your glove."

CHAPTER FIVE

Ollie was following Adam on his bike when Adam finally answered the question that Ollie had asked several times. "We're going to Gloria's house."

Ollie gulped. He didn't know what Adam had in mind, but whatever it was, there was no way it was going to be a pleasant experience. "What are you—?"

"Just trust me," Adam said. "Just go along with whatever I do."

"Don't get in a fight with her, Adam. She'll knock the stuffing out of you."

"Don't worry. I'm not going to do anything like that."

But he didn't explain his plan, and Ollie was terrified.

When they reached Gloria's house, Ollie was

surprised. He had thought she might live in a tough neighborhood, maybe near the scrap yard. He expected a mean black dog outside, and maybe Jack Gibbs sitting on the porch, drinking beer and belching.

What he saw, though, was a pretty nice house, with roses by the front porch. A pleasant-looking woman, who he figured was Gloria's mother, answered the door. "Is Gloria here?" Adam asked.

"Yes. But she's practicing the piano right now. She can't play baseball—or any other kind of ball—until she's finished."

Ollie wanted to see that: Gloria playing the piano.

"How long?" Adam asked.

Mrs. Gibbs looked at her watch. "Twenty more minutes."

"Okay. But don't tell her that two tall, weird-looking guys are out here. Just say, 'Someone wants to . . .' Well, just ask her not to get mad or . . . never mind. Don't say any of that. We'll wait, but please don't tip her off who's here."

The woman smiled, as though she understood. And then she said, "Okay. Twenty minutes."

Adam and Ollie sat on the porch and waited. Ollie was still nervous, and now he could see that Adam was, too. Ollie hoped that piano music would put Gloria in a good mood, but it didn't seem likely.

In a couple of minutes a dented old pickup truck pulled up in front of the house, and a guy in greasy coveralls climbed out. It wasn't Jack Gibbs, but it was a younger version of him: a huge kid, with massive shoulders, who hadn't shaved for a few days. This had to be Gloria's big brother.

The guy seemed to be headed past the house to the garage or the backyard when he spotted Adam and Ollie. He stopped in his tracks and stared at them. "What do you two want?" he asked.

"We're waiting for Gloria," Adam said—or sort of whispered.

The big guy grinned, showing some rusty teeth. "Do you *love* her?" he asked, and then he laughed at a volume that could set off tidal waves.

He didn't wait for the boys to answer. "You're both ugly," he said. "You look about right for Gloria. But don't start trying to kiss her." He pointed a grimy finger at Adam and then at Ollie. "If you do, I'll break all four of those toothpick legs of yours."

He turned and marched away.

Adam mumbled, "We only play baseball with her," but not loud enough for the departing giant to hear.

"Let's get out of here," Ollie said.

"No. Hang on. We'll be all right."

But the minutes passed slowly, and by the time Gloria stepped onto the porch, Ollie was a nervous wreck. Things didn't improve when Gloria took one look at him and Adam and said, "What do *you* want?"

Adam stood up. "Hi, Gloria," he said. "How did your piano practice go?"

"Look, don't get smart with me, Adam," Gloria barked. "My mom makes me take piano. It's not my idea."

"A lot of kids take piano lessons. There's nothing wrong with that."

"What are you doing here?" Gloria was actually dressed rather nicely this morning. She had on clean jeans, with no rips or holes, and a white

T-shirt. Her short hair even looked brushed. But none of that changed the way she sounded. Whatever Adam had in mind, Ollie was sure it had been a mistake.

"You know how you said yesterday that me and Ollie can't pitch very well?"

"Sure. What about it?"

"Well . . . since the coach still wants us to pitch, and you're right—we really aren't very good—we wondered if you would give us some help?"

"*What?*"

Ollie was surprised by Adam's request, but Gloria was clearly *astounded*. She kept looking from Adam to Ollie as though she were trying to figure out what they were really up to.

"You're such a good player," Adam said, "and you mentioned that you had pitched before. We just thought maybe you had noticed what we were doing wrong yesterday."

"Look, I'm not much of a teacher."

"But you know a lot more than we do," Adam said, in a quiet voice, still sounding friendly. "I just thought that we could throw some pitches to you, and you could watch what we're doing. Maybe you can spot something in our motions—or something like that. We both need to improve our control."

Now Gloria was standing with her mouth open a little, her eyes still as rivets.

"Would you mind?"

"You want to throw pitches to me? And then hear what I have to say about your pitching?"

"Yes."

"Well . . . whatever," she said, in a sort of gasp. Then she turned and walked into the house.

As the screen door slammed, Ollie said, "What the heck are you trying to do, Adam?"

"You heard me."

"Yeah, but you're up to something."

"Just keep going along with me. I think this is going to work."

Gloria was at the door again, and she had her baseball glove with her. Without saying a word, she walked to the driveway and motioned for the boys to head toward the other end, near the street. She stopped in front of the garage. "Did you birdbrains think to bring a ball?" she said.

"Sure." Adam went to his bike and got his glove and ball and then stood at the end of the driveway. "Is this about the right distance?" he asked.

"You tell me. You're the pitcher."

"I think it's about right."

"Good. Throw the ball. I don't have all day."

Adam took his position, as though he were placing his foot on a pitching rubber. He wound up and threw a soft pitch, just a warm-up throw. Gloria caught it, and then she tossed it back, quickly. "Throw a few more easy ones like that," she said, "and then pick up your speed a little at a time."

Adam chucked the ball faster with each pitch until he was firing hard. And most of his pitches would have been strikes. After about ten throws, Gloria said, "There's nothing wrong with your motion. Why don't you throw like that in the games?"

"It just seems like we're playing catch out here," Adam said. "But in a game, I start worrying about walking guys, and then I mess up."

"Look, both of you guys try too hard to hit corners. In this league, if you can get the ball over the plate with something on it, that's good enough. Batters may put the ball in play, but the defense can help you out."

"Yeah. I guess that's right," Adam said, sounding like he appreciated the advice.

"Throw me some breaking pitches," Gloria said.

For the next few minutes, she called for different pitches, and she did pick up some minor problems in Adam's delivery. She told him he was changing his motion on his curve, so the batter could see immediately that it wasn't a fastball. Sometimes he was turning his shoulders too much, too, trying to reach back for extra power. "The biggest mistake you can make is to force the ball. You said when we started that you felt like you were playing catch. That's how pitching ought to feel. It's okay to throw hard, but never aim and never overthrow. Just look at your target and play catch."

Adam popped another nice fastball into her glove, and she said, "Nice pitch. You didn't look like you were throwing all that hard, but you had good speed on the ball. Most guys will swing and miss at a pitch like that, especially if you keep it down in the strike zone, the way you did that time."

"All right. Thanks. That felt really good. Let Ollie throw some now."

Ollie took the ball and stepped to the spot where Adam had been pitching. He was about to wind up for his first toss when Gloria said, "Aren't you going to start talking now and tell me what's coming?"

Adam said, "He's trying not to do that."

"Good luck," Gloria said. Ollie knew she didn't think he could do it. The sad part was, Ollie didn't think so either. He kept his mouth shut, but his pitches were all over the place.

Gloria saw some of the reasons. Ollie wasn't consistent. His motion would change with each pitch, and he was letting his shoulder drop sometimes, so that he wasn't bringing his arm over the top. "Remember what I told Adam," she instructed him. "Throw hard, but pretend you're playing catch with me."

"I can't do that," Ollie whispered to himself.

"What are you doing, talking to yourself again?"

His next pitch was way over her head. It banged against the garage, and from the backyard Gloria's big brother shouted, "Hey, watch what you kids are doing out there."

"Shut up, Dale," Gloria yelled back at her brother. "I'm trying to teach this numskull how to pitch, and it ain't easy." She was chasing the ball down.

"Oh, sure—like you know anything about it yourself," Dale yelled.

"I know a lot more than you do—or ever will."

"Hey, watch your tongue, or I'll put you in my vise and tighten it down on you."

The insults continued for a time, and all the fuss was only raising Ollie's anxiety. "Just forget about all that stuff," he whispered to himself. "Think about playing catch. Concentrate on that."

And he threw a good fastball.

Gloria caught it and for a few seconds stayed in her crouch. Then she stood up but didn't throw the ball back. Instead, she walked up the driveway to Ollie. When she reached him, she said, "What did you just say to yourself?"

"What you told me. To think about playing catch."

"And it helped that much, to say it?"

"Yeah. I guess."

"Why does that work for you?"

"I don't know. There's always so much noise. My voice helps shut it out."

"Why do you listen to the noise?"

That was an interesting question. Ollie had never thought he had any choice. "Everyone yells at me when I'm pitching," Ollie said. "I can't help hearing it."

"Hey, don't listen to any of that stuff," Gloria said. "If I'm up to bat and guys are yelling that I can't get a hit, I just laugh. I shut everything out, and then I look for that ball and slam it somewhere."

"It's hard for me to do that."

"Don't be such a wimp. Just know you can do it, and do it."

Adam was standing a little way off, but now he stepped up close. "It's one thing to shut out what guys on other teams say, but it's harder when you think your own teammates don't believe in you."

Gloria spun toward Adam. "That's why you came over here, isn't it? That's what you wanted to say to me."

"We wanted to get your help. You already helped me a lot."

Gloria stood for a long time with her hands on her hips. She seemed to be trying to decide whether to be mad or not. Finally, she turned back toward Ollie. "Don't talk to yourself when you're pitching. If you'll do that, I won't say anything to you either."

"Okay."

"You have a good arm, Ollie. Now throw me some pitches, and don't worry what *anybody* thinks. Just do what you know you can do."

"All right."

Ollie took the ball and began to throw—better than he had in a long time. Maybe he *could* pitch. Maybe he wouldn't have to quit after all.

CHAPTER SIX

The Scrappers' next game was against the Pit Bulls—a team that had beaten them the last time they played. The Scrappers really needed to come back and play well this time. They had to get some momentum going before they moved into the second half of the season.

Practices had been all right. Gloria had been quieter than usual, and she hadn't bothered Ollie. In fact, she had even cheered him on.

The only problem was, everyone seemed down. Maybe they were remembering how badly they had gotten beaten in the last game. Ollie thought they had given up on themselves. Of course, he understood that. He was trying to remember everything Gloria had shown him, but he still was nervous about going back out on the mound.

At least he didn't have to pitch this next game. It was Adam's turn.

Then the coach stopped him after practice. "I know you pitched more than Adam last time," he told Ollie, "but I want you to pitch against the Pit Bulls tomorrow. You need to prove to yourself you can throw the way you did earlier in the season."

Ollie looked down at the grass. He felt almost sick.

"Look at me, Ollie," the coach said, and Ollie looked up. "You have the capability to be a *great* pitcher. You can do a lot more with a baseball than most kids your age. If you ever start believing in yourself, you'll be unstoppable."

Ollie nodded. He tried to accept the idea, but the doubts wouldn't go away. He thought again about telling the coach he would rather quit, but he couldn't forget what his mom had told him about letting down the whole team. And he couldn't forget how good it had felt pitching in Gloria's driveway.

Ollie was tense all the next day, and when he took his warm-up pitches before the game, the ball was flying all over the place. He was trying hard to imagine that he was just playing catch with Wilson, but he was sure the team was expecting another disaster, and it was hard to put that out of his mind.

Ollie was also trying hard not to talk to himself. The coach had worked with him at practice. "Think what you want," he had said. "Tell yourself whatever you need to hear. Just do it *inside* your head." It was the same thing Gloria had said, and Ollie knew they were both right.

The first batter was a kid named Waxman. He was fast, but he was no great hitter. The guy would do almost anything to get a walk—and then steal second and third.

So Ollie told himself—inside his head—to get the ball over the plate. Waxman wouldn't swing at the first couple of pitches anyway.

Ollie did everything right on the first pitch. He didn't throw too hard. He didn't try to hit the corners. He just chucked the ball down the middle. Or at least, that's what he meant to do. But the ball came in hard and low.

So he tried to bring the next one up, and he did—way up.

When Ollie got the ball back, he turned with

his back to the batter and said, in his mind, *Okay. Stop that. Just throw the ball to Wilson—like you're playing catch. Waxman won't swing.*

It was a great idea, but when he turned around, everything changed. He fired the ball hard again. And low again.

And then high again.

Ollie was furious at himself. He had actually walked Waxman on four pitches—a guy who had no bat at all.

Don't worry about Waxman, he thought. But he did worry—a lot. He could see everything falling apart, just the way it had in the last game.

Ollie checked Waxman carefully, wound up, and just as his arm started forward, he saw the guy take off. He tried to hurry the pitch, and he bounced the ball in the dirt. Wilson didn't even make a throw. Waxman had the steal, all the way.

Gloria ran over to the mound. "Ollie, you're forcing your pitches," she said. "You're aiming the ball. Remember what I told you. Just act like you're playing catch, and throw the ball to Wilson. Don't let Waxman worry you."

Ollie nodded. But why couldn't he get his arm to understand what his head knew?

He did get one called strike, but he walked the batter, Wayment, on five pitches.

Sweat started breaking out all over him.

The Pit Bulls were standing up in the dugout, screaming and yelling. "Ollie, Ollie, in free," someone kept saying. "Don't swing, Lumps. He'll walk you."

And up in the crowd, some big guy—someone's dad—kept yelling, "Hey, kid, you couldn't throw a strike right now if your life depended on it."

Ollie was willing to do anything to throw a strike, even if the next batter—"Lumps" Lanman—hit it a mile.

Ollie eased way off, tried to throw a nice, soft pitch that Lumps would at least swing at.

And it almost happened. But the ball had so little speed on it that it dropped in front of the plate.

Ollie put more mustard on the next one and really popped Wilson's glove—but way outside.

This couldn't be happening again.

The noise was getting worse and worse. People were screaming at Ollie from the bench and the bleachers, and his own players were yelling their support—but with a tone that said, "Please don't do this to us again."

Ollie took a deep breath, tried to think of nothing at all, and just threw the ball to the catcher's mitt. It would have been a perfect pitch had the catcher's mitt been on the batter's ear. But it wasn't, and Lumps almost got a lump.

Instead, he hit the dirt and came up screaming, "Give me something I can hit, Ollie, and I'll knock you off that mound."

That actually sounded like a good idea. An injury would be better than this.

When the pitch sailed high again and the ump said, "Take your base," Ollie was relieved. The bases were loaded, but at least Coach Carlton was walking to the mound. Adam, or maybe Thurlow, would be taking over now.

"Ollie, what's bothering you?" the coach asked.

"I don't know. I can't make the ball do what I want it to."

"Can you go back to talking to yourself, and just keep your voice down? Maybe cover up your mouth with your glove?"

"I don't know. My voice forgets to be quiet sometimes."

"Well . . . try it. I think I got you messed up by telling you not to talk to yourself."

"Okay."

Ollie immediately felt better. As soon as the coach walked away, he whispered, "All right, I'm back." Then he concentrated on Wilson's glove, and he told himself—with his glove over his mouth—"Just see the pitch you want to throw."

This batter was a lefty, a boy named Clark Krieger, and he was leaning in toward the plate. Ollie visualized a pitch on the inside edge—a good, hard fastball.

Ollie took his stretch and checked the runners. And now the picture was in his mind.

Ollie's release felt good. The ball whizzed close to the batter—a little more inside than Ollie had wanted.

Krieger ducked away. As he did, his bat accidentally swung toward the plate. The ball glanced off the bat and rolled onto the grass.

Wilson charged out, grabbed the ball, and then hustled back to step on the plate. Even Waxman, fast as he was, couldn't get there ahead of him.

One away. And Ollie felt a whole lot better.

Now a guy named Scott Johnson was stepping up to the plate. "Throw *me* that pitch," he called to Ollie. He licked his lips.

Johnson took a couple of slick practice strokes. "He's going to look so stupid when he strikes out," Ollie said, with the glove over his face. "I see the ball at his knees, and hard."

Ollie tossed a perfect pitch—the one he had described to himself. Johnson took a hard swing and missed.

The Pit Bulls seemed surprised that Ollie could find his control. They weren't yelling so much now. But Ollie's own teammates were going crazy. "Now you've got it going," Gloria yelled, and Ollie liked her confidence.

"Go with your curve," Ollie whispered, and Wilson was thinking the same thing. Ollie nodded to the signal, and then he snapped off a curve that broke over the heart of the plate—just as Johnson was backing away.

"*Steeeeriiiiiike!*"

"Now your hard stuff. Bust him down the middle." The voice was clear and so was the picture. Ollie threw a good fastball over the plate.

Johnson took a huge cut at it . . . and missed.

"Strike *three*. You're out!" the ump barked.

Johnson tossed his bat away. He wasn't talking now, wasn't even looking at Ollie.

"This is getting to be fun," Ollie told himself. "This next guy doesn't look like a hitter. Throw him some good fastballs, and this inning will be over for the Bulls."

That was almost what happened. Ollie threw a fastball down the middle, and the hitter, a boy named Egan, slapped it in the air. Trent and Jeremy both raced hard to get to it, but then, at the last second, both backed away.

The ball dropped between them.

The runners had been off with the pitch, and they were really rolling by the time the ball hit the grass. Jeremy chased down the ball and threw hard. But he had no chance to get Krieger, who had rounded the bases and come all the way from first.

Three runs had scored on a fly ball that should have been caught.

It was a tense moment. Ollie watched Gloria. She socked her glove a couple of times. She spit in the dirt. Then she walked back to her position.

She didn't say a word to Trent or Jeremy.

The coach was yelling, "Trent, Jeremy—someone has to call for that ball."

Both nodded. Ollie knew they felt dumb. It wasn't like either one of them to make a mistake like that.

Ollie told himself, "It's all right. Just throw a good pitch. Get this inning over with."

Wilson put down one finger, and Ollie whispered, with the glove over his mouth, "Blow a fastball past him." He pictured the ball slamming into Wilson's glove.

He took a breath, relaxed, and tossed the ball hard.

Sarah Pollick, the batter, spanked a weak grounder to the right side. Tracy had to charge the ball, but she scooped it up and threw to Adam.

The ball was there in time, and the Scrappers were off the field.

As the players ran back to the dugout, everyone yelled to Tracy that she had made a good play.

And back at the dugout, Gloria sat down next to Jeremy. Ollie heard her say, calmly, "Jeremy, the center fielder has to be the leader in the outfield. If you know you can make the catch, you have to scream it out, loud and clear, and call everyone else off."

"Yeah, I know," Jeremy said. "I was worried about catching the ball, and I didn't think about anything else."

"Yeah, well, it's easy to do something like that."

No one got mad. Ollie was amazed. He could tell that Gloria was trying to be a leader, not a complainer. Maybe she had learned something from the little visit Adam and Ollie had made to her house.

Things were looking up. But now the Scrappers had to get those runs back. They were already down 3 to 0.

CHAPTER SEVEN

Jeremy stepped to the plate. Trent yelled, "All right, let's get it going!"

Tony Gomez, the Pit Bulls' pitcher, was high with his first two pitches. But when Jeremy got a pitch in the strike zone, he knocked the ball up the middle. It looked like a sure base hit, but Johnson darted to his right and stabbed the ball.

Jeremy ran hard, but he couldn't beat the throw. Tough luck.

Robbie's luck was better. He hit a slow grounder to third, but Lanman hurried his throw and pulled the first baseman off the bag. Robbie was safe.

Now the Scrappers began to whoop it up.

As Gloria walked to the plate, one of the Pit Bulls yelled to Gomez, "Hey, Tony, don't let this *girl* scare you. She just looks mean."

Gloria gave the guy a hard stare, but she dug in and got ready. The first pitch was belt high, and she took a smooth, natural swing. The ball darted into right center and rolled between the outfielders.

Robbie was going all out, thinking he might score, but the coach threw his arms up, and Robbie stopped at third.

Gloria had rounded second by then, and she had to throw on her brakes and scamper back to the bag. At least she had looked to get the coach's signal.

Ollie knew that she had been thinking triple all the way, and she didn't like to be stopped. She walked back to the bag and kicked it, but she didn't say anything.

Thurlow was up next, and the Pit Bulls knew what a great hitter he was. With first base open, Gomez didn't throw a pitch that Thurlow could swing at. Everything was outside—four pitches in a row.

Thurlow trotted to first base. And once he got there, he took a careful lead. He seemed to be paying attention today.

Now the bases were loaded, and Wilson, another power hitter, was up. But he was way too eager. He swung at a pitch that was almost in the dirt. He made contact, but he only managed to scoot a grounder toward Waxman at shortstop.

Waxman scooped the ball up and ran to second. He stepped on the bag for the force-out and then threw to first.

Wilson could run pretty well for a big guy, and he beat the throw—just barely.

The run scored from third, but now there were two outs. It was Tracy who had to keep things going.

Tracy took a couple of pitches, high, and then Gomez came down the middle with a fast-ball. She stroked it past the second baseman for a base hit. Gloria scored, and Wilson stopped at second.

The rally was still on.

And now Trent was up.

His hitting had been improving lately, but he was no slugger. Gloria yelled from the dugout, "Come on, Trent. You can do it."

But Trent hit a fly ball that sailed high toward left. Egan took it in, and the inning was over. The score was 3 to 2, with the Pit Bulls ahead.

Ollie saw Gloria slam her glove against her leg. But she didn't say anything. She got up and headed out to her position.

Coach Carlton was clapping his hands. "All right, kids," he said. "Let's play some defense."

And that's what they did. For the next two innings, no one scored on either side, but the Scrappers made some good plays. Thurlow ran down a long fly in right that could have gone for extra bases. And Tracy raced straight back on a high pop-up, spun around, and made a nice catch.

"Hey," Coach Carlton called out, after the top of the fourth inning, "we're playing some baseball now. We're looking good."

Ollie was pleased by the good defense. But his pitching still wasn't as sharp as he wanted it to be. Describing his pitches to himself had helped a lot, but he still didn't have the burning speed he had had at times earlier in the season. He had been lucky not to give up any more runs.

When he sat down on the bench this time, Gloria sat down next to him. "Ollie, you're still forcing your pitches a little too much," she said. "You do all right until you get in a tight spot.

Then you start muscling the ball. That cuts your speed."

Ollie knew that, but he was so pumped up he couldn't seem to relax and let the ball fly.

"Don't be so serious about it," Thurlow said.

Ollie was surprised. He turned toward Thurlow and said, "What?"

"Don't think so much. Just throw."

It was probably pretty good advice, but the most important thing was that it had come from Thurlow. "Yeah. You're right," Ollie said. "That's what I need to do."

But his insides were still churning.

Ollie did feel a little calmer when he took the mound in the fifth inning—even though the Scrappers still hadn't gotten anything going and the score remained 3 to 2.

He made a good pitch that fooled Lanman. But Lumps got lucky. He flicked his bat out and sent a slow roller down the first base line: an accidental bunt. No one could get to it in time, and Lanman ended up on first.

Krieger was up now. Ollie wound up and threw a good pitch to him. Krieger swung a little late, but he hammered a line drive up the right field line. The ball landed in fair territory and rolled toward the corner. Thurlow ran a long way to get to the ball, and he made a good throw to Tracy. But big Lanman had charged all the way around the bases and was headed home.

Tracy spun and fired a strike to Wilson. Wilson was blocking the plate, and he got his tag down just right. But Lumps slid hard into Wilson. When the dust cleared, Wilson hadn't moved much, but the ball was in the dirt.

"Safe!" the umpire shouted. Another run had scored.

"What do you mean 'safe'?" Gloria yelled, charging toward home plate.

The ump pointed to the ball on the ground. Wilson reached down and picked it up.

"He didn't drop it until after the play," Gloria shouted. "I saw him put the tag on the runner. You saw it, too, and you know it."

"Young lady, that's enough. Just play ball."

"How can we, when you won't give us a fighting chance?"

"One more crack, and you're out of here." The umpire, with his chest protector hanging over his arm, stepped toward her.

By now, Coach Carlton was hurrying toward home plate. "Gloria, get back to your position," he called to her.

"Wilson put the tag on him, Coach. Didn't you see it?"

But Wilson said, "His foot hit my glove. It knocked the ball out."

Gloria was left with nothing to say. She twirled around and marched away, but Ollie was worried. He had the feeling Gloria could go ballistic at any moment.

Fortunately, Ollie got Johnson out on a pop-up that Adam caught in foul territory. And Gloria began to talk it up again. "Good catch, Adam," she said. Ollie knew she was trying hard to get herself back under control.

Ollie was still struggling. He threw three straight balls to Egan, and then he had a good talk with himself—told himself to relax. On his next pitch, his motion felt better, and so did his follow-through.

But the umpire called it ball four.

It had been *so* close—right at Egan's knees.

Ollie glanced at Gloria, who looked disgusted. "Come on, Ollie," she said. "Just throw strikes."

It wasn't anything too terrible, but it was a step in the wrong direction. Ollie wondered what the coach would do.

But it was Tracy who said, "Don't start that again, Gloria."

Gloria answered, a little louder this time, "Don't start *what?*"

"Gloria." This was from the coach.

Gloria ducked her head and chomped on her gum.

Ollie felt the tension. He whispered to himself, "You're okay. Remember what Thurlow said. Don't be so serious." But he couldn't get himself to believe his own words. He could only think of that stupid strike zone that had become hard to hit again.

He threw a pitch to Pollick that hit in the dirt and then bounced off Wilson's chest protector.

The runners on first and third each bluffed a move, but Wilson came out ready to throw, and they held up.

Gloria kicked at the dirt. And then she said what she must have been thinking all along. "Coach, let me pitch. I can throw strikes."

"Time-out," Mr. Carlton shouted. He walked

to the mound, and he waved for Gloria to come over. "Gloria," he said, when she reached him, "are you going to start again? How many times do I have to talk to you about this?"

"Hey, the only thing I'm saying is that I can throw strikes. Ollie can't get the ball over the plate right now. You can see that. If you don't want me to pitch, put Thurlow in."

"Do you think you're supporting Ollie when you say things like that?"

Gloria held back for a moment, but then she said, "I'm supporting my team. If we want to win, we need a pitcher who can get somebody out."

"Gloria, you're out of this game. I want you to go to the bench and tell Cindy to come in and play shortstop. And then I want you to sit in that dugout and cheer for the team."

"Oh, come on, Coach. All I'm—"

"Either sit on the bench or go home. But if you go home, I'll drop you off our roster, and we'll play the rest of the season without you. Some people think you're the problem on this team. Maybe they're right."

Gloria spun away and walked off the field. As

she reached the foul line, she kicked her glove, like a football, all the way to the dugout.

The coach was looking at Ollie. "You've had your ups and downs today," he said, "but I've never really seen your best motion. I guess whispering to yourself hasn't helped much."

"It did at first. But I don't know what's wrong now. Nothing feels right."

"Tell me this," the coach said. "When you talk out loud, who are you talking to?"

"Me."

"Have you ever tried talking to the ball instead?"

"What?"

"Why don't you just tell the ball what you want it to do. Hold it up to your mouth and explain to it, very quietly, where it's supposed to go."

Ollie smiled. "I don't think baseballs listen very well," he said.

"What are you talking about? That baseball wants to do the right thing. It just isn't sure what you want right now."

Ollie didn't believe that, of course. But he liked the idea. The ball really ought to take some responsibility for what it did. The thing had been going off on its own all day.

So as the coach walked away, Ollie stepped on the pitching rubber and held the ball close to his lips. "All right, fly straight to Wilson's mitt. And show a little pop for a change."

Ollie smiled at the idea. But it was nice to put the responsibility on the ball—and not think so much about what he had to do. He stretched and fired—and the pitch was a rocket.

The umpire called, "Strike one," and Ollie laughed. The ball had listened.

Ollie took Wilson's sign. Fastball, again. "This time, go over there where Wilson's setting up. Down and away from the batter. And, hey, don't waste your time getting there."

Wham! The ball did it. Pollick swung hard, but she missed.

Now Ollie was laughing. "Hey, this works," he said. "But listen," he told the ball, "Wilson wants a curve. I'm going to give you some spin, so don't get lost."

He threw the ball, and it knew what it was doing. It bent to the center of the plate just as Pollick bailed out.

"Strike three!"

Ollie heard his teammates shout, and he heard his dad yell, "Now you're chucking."

Ollie looked at Gloria. She was sitting with her arms folded. She looked mad enough to eat the bench she was sitting on. And she *wasn't* cheering for her team.

But Ollie couldn't worry about that. He just hoped the ball would keep listening to him. "Okay, show some pep. Right at the knees. This kid is going to swing, but he can't hit you."

The ball did its thing, and Gomez took an awkward swing. He got a piece of the ball, but he rolled it straight to Ollie. Ollie picked it up and said, "Nice job. Go to Adam, now." He waited until Adam had set up at first, and then *bam*, the throw was there, and the top of the inning was over. The Scrappers were down by only two runs—4 to 2—when it might have been a lot worse.

When Ollie ran back to the dugout, everyone was yelling for him. But Ollie was worried about Gloria. She was sitting at the end of the dugout, leaning back, with her feet up on the fence.

Ollie took a chance. He walked all the way down to her, stood, and waited. Still, she wouldn't glance up at him. "It was no big deal," he said.

"Why didn't you throw like that when I was out there?" she said, without looking at him. "Then I'd still be in the game."

"The coach helped me. He told me to talk to the ball. So I told the ball what it was supposed to do, and it did it."

She looked up. "You've got a screw loose, Ollie. I swear you do."

"It worked."

"How am I supposed to keep my mouth shut when I'm playing with a loony tune like you?"

She looked away, and Ollie was going to let the whole thing go. But Tracy said, "Hey, you're the one who causes all the bad feelings on this team."

"Shut up, Tracy," Gloria said, "or I'll show you some bad feelings all over your nose."

"You don't get it, do you?" Tracy said. "You don't know what it means to be part of a team."

Gloria didn't answer.

CHAPTER EIGHT

The Scrappers needed some runs. Tony Gomez was a pretty good pitcher but not overpowering. The Scrappers just hadn't been able to put hits together or get a big hit with runners on base. But things started well in the bottom of the fifth. Wilson hit an easy grounder toward second, and Johnson let the ball slip under his glove and through his legs.

Wilson stood on first, grinning, and he yelled, "Come on, Tracy. Smack a long shot—just like I did."

Coach Carlton was saying the opposite. "Just meet the ball, Tracy. Let's get something going."

Tracy nodded. And she seemed to listen. She let a high pitch go by, and then she took a good stroke at a fastball. She drove a line shot up the middle.

The ball got to center field quickly. The fielder made a quick throw back to the infield, so Wilson stopped at second.

This was a good chance for some runs—two runners on base with no outs. But Trent was up, and Chad, now in the game for Adam, was on deck. Ollie was in the hole. That was not exactly the tough part of the lineup.

Trent swung hard at the first pitch and rolled a grounder toward third. Nothing much seemed likely to come from that.

Lumps Lanman, playing third, charged the ball. He grabbed it and then spun around. But the shortstop hadn't covered, and Lumps had no chance to get back to the bag in time. By then, it was also too late to make the long throw to get Trent.

Now the bases were loaded, with no outs.

The Scrappers were up and yelling.

It was the Pit Bulls who were upset with their own players. Gomez shouted, "What were you thinking, Lumps? Wake up out there!"

"Ah, shut up," Lanman said. "Waxman's the one who messed up."

Ollie was on deck, so he got up and walked out to the bat rack. He glanced at Gloria, who was now sitting up, taking this all in. Ollie hoped she noticed how stupid it sounded when teammates yelled at one another.

Chad didn't get as lucky as everyone else had been. He chopped a ball back to the pitcher, and Gomez came home with it. Wilson was forced at home.

The bases were still loaded, but now there was one out. Maybe another rally was going to die.

Ollie felt almost sick. He didn't want to bat in such a crucial situation. He heard his dad shout, "Poke it somewhere, Ollie. Get a hit!" And all the kids in the dugout were pleading with him to come through.

Ollie hoped maybe he could wait out the pitcher and get a walk. Why not make some other pitcher sweat it out for a change?

The first pitch was big as a planet, and it rotated right through the strike zone. Ollie let it go by, and then he felt like an idiot.

But he felt even worse when the next pitch was a foot outside and he took a wild swing at it.

The Pit Bull infielders liked what they were seeing, and all of them were talking it up now: "Ollie's going to *whiff*. Just throw one more by him."

Ollie stepped out of the box, held up his hand, and said, "Time-out."

He needed to get rid of the noise in his head and just watch the ball. "Bat," he said, "*you* make the decision. If it's a good pitch, swing. But not too hard. Just jump out there and give that ball a sweet kiss."

Ollie stepped back in, but he heard the catcher say, "You're not at all normal, you know that, Ollie? You not only talk to yourself; you talk to bats and balls."

Ollie had to laugh. If the kid only knew what a relief it was to let the bats and balls take over and play this game.

The pitch was outside again. And the bat made a good decision. It stayed put.

It did the same on the next pitch.

Now the noise was furious, but Ollie didn't let it get to him. He trusted his bat.

Gomez delivered his next pitch—letter high and hard—and the bat leaped out to meet it.

Ping! The sound of solid aluminum. The ball shot like a javelin into left field.

Two runs scored, and the game was tied.

Ollie didn't show off. But he looked up at his parents and smiled. Then he looked at Gloria. She was standing up now, clapping. She wasn't going wild—Wanda was doing that for her—but she was starting to get back into the game.

The top of the batting order was coming up. Jeremy, as he often did, punched a little hit into right field. No one scored, but the bases were loaded again.

Then Robbie hit a liner to right center. The right fielder ran hard, but he couldn't get to it. He made a good relay, but Ollie ran his heart out, slid hard, and got under Lanman's tag at third. Chad had scored ahead of him.

The Scrappers were getting scrappy, and now they had a one-run lead, 5 to 4. In the dugout, all the kids were going crazy. They were yelling and high-fiving and shouting for Cindy to keep it going.

Gloria was still standing up, watching. Ollie knew it was killing her not to be batting right now. And she must have felt even worse when Cindy struck out. Ollie saw Gloria drop down on the bench. But she didn't kick anything; she stared straight into the dirt.

The rest of the kids were yelling for Thurlow to go for the fence. Thurlow didn't act as though he heard a word, but he took a good stance.

He swung on the first pitch—at a ball that was probably outside—and he didn't quite get it all.

But he got enough.

He stroked a drive past the second baseman. The ball sliced toward the line. It got past the right fielder and rolled to the corner.

Three more runs scored.

Thurlow didn't seem to be running that hard, but he cruised around the bases, *fast*, and might have had a chance at an inside-the-park homer if the coach hadn't stopped him at third.

"Way to go, Thurlow!" someone was yelling. Ollie heard that raspy voice and looked to be sure. It *was* Gloria.

Thurlow was still acting as though he didn't hear. But he looked pleased, and he watched the action intently, ready to go if Wilson made contact.

But Wilson got a little too anxious. He swung at some bad pitches and ended up striking out.

Finally, the inning was over.

"Let's play defense," everyone was screaming, and Ollie felt the change. He heard the excitement and the confidence, but he also felt the friendship. Everyone was having a great time. It wasn't just that they were playing well. They were supporting one another.

They were ahead 8 to 4, and just about everyone had gotten in on the act.

Ollie knew he needed to pitch well. Or at least the ball needed to do its job.

When he got to the mound, he explained to the ball that things were different now. It had been all right to hit the bat when the Scrappers had been up, but it shouldn't do that now.

Ollie felt good when he threw the first pitch, and the ball did behave itself. But the bat had ideas of its own. The bat and ball connected, and the ball shot toward left center.

Jeremy and Trent both took off after it, but Jeremy was screaming as loud as he could, "I've got it. I've got it."

Trent changed his angle and moved into a position to back Jeremy up. Jeremy reached up and snagged the ball. Then he looked at Trent and grinned.

One away.

The next batter, Waxman, stroked a grounder to the right side. Tracy got in front of the ball, but it skipped off her glove and rolled away. Still, she didn't panic. She ran to the ball, picked it up, set her feet, and made a good throw.

Smack!

The ball hit Chad's glove at about the same time the runner's foot struck the bag.

Ollie looked to the ump. He seemed to hesitate, but then his arm shot up. "Out!" he shouted.

The Pit Bulls yelled their complaints to the umpire. But he paid no attention.

Wayment, the next batter, hit a high bouncer to the left of the mound. Ollie ran a couple of steps and made a stab at it, but the ball got past him.

It bounced toward Cindy at short, but she didn't charge. She stayed back and caught the ball on a flat bounce that threw her off balance. By then, she was going to have to hurry. She forced a hard throw that hit in the dirt. Chad knocked it down, but he couldn't pick it up in time to get the runner.

"That's okay," Ollie told Cindy. He glanced at Gloria, and he knew how bad she felt that she wasn't playing in that spot. But Gloria shouted, "Don't worry about it, Cindy. That was a tough one."

Ollie laughed. Was that really Gloria talking?

Cindy's play worried Ollie, though. The one way the Pit Bulls could get back in the game would be for the Scrappers to start making mistakes. Lanman was coming up, and he could hit the ball a mile.

"Okay, no problem," Ollie told the ball. "But let's get a strikeout this time. Stay outside, just a little. Maybe he'll chase one."

Ollie concentrated on the target, and the ball did pretty well—except that it ended up a little more outside than Ollie might have liked. Lanman didn't swing.

"Okay, maybe I asked too much of you. Let's get back to basics and hit the plate for a strike."

The next pitch was a strike, and in a pretty good spot. But Lanman got around on it, and he jerked it right at Cindy again.

Ollie was afraid another disaster might be coming.

But Cindy got low, just the way the coach always told the kids to do. The ball rolled right into her glove and stuck.

And now all she had to worry about was the short throw to second.

But Cindy wasn't thinking. She tossed the ball all the way to first.

"Second!" Ollie was yelling, too late, but he spun toward first base—just as the ball popped into Chad's glove.

Chad hadn't expected the throw, and he had to catch the ball and then reach with his foot to make the tag. But he did that in plenty of time.

And the side was retired.

"Hey, Cindy!" Gloria was screaming. "You're a shortstop!"

Ollie ran to Cindy and slammed her on the back.

Cindy had never looked so happy all season.

Ollie decided to wait until a little later to remind her that the throw to second for the force would have been a whole lot easier.

The important thing was, the Scrappers still held their four-run lead.

CHAPTER NINE

The Scrappers didn't score in the bottom of the sixth inning. But as the final inning, the seventh, began, the score was still 8 to 4. Ollie was throwing pretty well now, and the team was playing great defense. All the Scrappers had to do was get three outs—and they had that four-run cushion to work with.

Ollie stood on the mound and got the sign from Wilson, who wanted to do something different and start with a curveball. "Got that?" Ollie asked the ball. "He wants you to do your bend thing. I'll do my part, you do the rest."

Ollie was about to start his motion when he heard a loud "Time-out!" Mr. Snyder, the Pit Bulls' coach, was walking toward the umpire. "I think that kid is wetting down the ball," he yelled. "He puts it up to his mouth every time he pitches."

Ollie didn't wait. He jogged toward the place where the coach and the ump were about to meet each other. "I don't spit on it or anything. I just talk to it. There's no rule against that."

"What do you mean, you *talk* to it?" Snyder asked.

"I tell the ball what to do. I can do that all I want. Ask my coach."

Coach Carlton was now walking toward the others. As he approached, he said, "He certainly can talk to the ball. Mark Fidrych used to do it in the major leagues. No one ever told him that he couldn't."

"I think he's spitting on the ball," Mr. Snyder said. "Either that, or he's breathing real hard, and getting vapor on it. Something like that. The ball is doing stuff now that it wasn't before he started putting it up to his mouth."

"The ball knows what to do now. That's all," Ollie said. He grinned at Coach Carlton.

The coach said, "That's exactly right. Don't you tell your pitchers to talk to the ball? I saw Ollie talk to his bat—and that worked, too."

Mr. Snyder looked confused. He was a hefty

guy. His blue Pit Bulls shirt was stretched tight under his arms and over his big middle. "What are you trying to pull?" he asked, looking Coach Carlton over as though he were some sort of crook.

"I'm not pulling anything."

"Well, it ain't right. Make a ruling, ump. He's teaching his kids to cheat."

The umpire took a long look at Coach Carlton, and then he said, "He can talk to the baseball all he wants, but he can't hold it up to his mouth. If he does, I'll call a ball each time he does it."

"Check that ball and see if he ain't done something to it already," Mr. Snyder said.

"Go right ahead," Coach Carlton said.

The umpire took the ball from Ollie. "It's fine," he said.

"Sure it is—*now*," the big coach said. "He's been standing there rubbing it around in his glove."

But the umpire ignored all that. "Just don't put it up to your mouth," he said. "Let's play ball."

So Ollie walked back to the mound. He took

his position, with his left foot on the rubber, and he looked to Wilson, who still wanted a curve. Krieger was up—a good hitter. "Okay, ball," Ollie said, holding it well away from his mouth. "You know what we said. We go with the curve."

But Wilson came flying out from behind the plate. "Wait a sec. Time-out." He ran to the mound. "Hey, Ollie," he said, "quiet down. I could hear you clear as anything—telling the ball to curve."

"Well, I've got to say it loud enough for the ball to hear."

"Come on, Ollie. You don't really think the ball can hear you, do you?" Wilson looked a little worried.

"The coach told me to talk to it. And it helps. But the ball has to hear what I'm saying."

"No. *You* have to hear what you're saying."

"Same thing."

"I don't think so, Ollie. If you think a ball can hear, you might want to go take a little rest for a while. You've had too much pressure on you."

Ollie knew Wilson was right—in a way. But

the ball *had* listened, or at least had seemed to. "Okay, okay," he said. "I'll say it softer."

"Whatever." Wilson shook his head and then trotted back to the plate.

Meanwhile, all the Pit Bulls were pouring it on. "Ollie's a nutcase. He's *wacko*," they were screaming. "He talks to baseballs."

This time Wilson signaled for a fastball. "Okay, partner," Ollie said, through his teeth. "You're on your way, ball. Go fast. And stay down around the knees."

But Ollie didn't feel good about all this anymore. It had been nice to think the ball could hear him. He knew it was only a trick, of course, but it had helped him. Now, he was on his own again.

He tossed the ball with good speed, but it didn't stay down. It was up in Krieger's power, and the guy smacked it hard.

The ball shot down the line in left, and Trent had to run a long way for it. Trent wasn't very fast, but he took a good angle to the ball, got to it as quickly as he could, and made a good throw. Krieger stopped at second.

Ollie felt tired. Maybe it was time to let

someone else try to get these last three outs. He looked at the coach.

"You're okay," the coach shouted. "Just throw strikes and we'll get these guys."

That was easy to say. But big Jackson, a sub for Johnson, was up. Ollie took a deep breath, and he didn't bother to tell the ball anything. He just threw.

He did get the ball over the plate, but Jackson teed off on it.

The ball ended up bouncing to the fence, between Trent and Jeremy. One run scored, and Jackson thundered all the way around to third.

Ollie looked at the coach again.

"Just get an out here, Ollie," he yelled. "Don't worry about the runner."

Ollie tried to think that way. But Ollie forced a pitch over the plate, and Egan pounded it into left field for a single.

Jackson scored, and now the lead was down to two. All the Pit Bulls were going wild, screaming and hollering. And most of the talk was the same kind of stuff: "What's the matter, Ollie? Won't the ball listen to you?"

Ollie's teammates were all telling him to hang in there.

Ollie could hardly think. He turned around, away from the batter, and tried to get his head on straight. "Ollie, don't listen to everybody," he told himself. "Just throw it over the plate." But he turned back and threw a pitch clear over Wilson's head.

At least it bounced off the backstop, and Wilson got it on the rebound. Egan had to stay at first.

Ollie knew he couldn't do that again. The batter was a sub who had come in for Pollick. Ollie really didn't think the guy was that great. So he aimed another pitch over the plate—and hoped.

The batter hit a hard shot to Cindy. It got to her so fast that Cindy stuck her glove out and looked away. The ball careened off her glove and rolled into left field. Egan stopped at second, but now the tying runs were on base.

All Ollie could think was that a ground ball like that might have been a perfect double-play ball—if only Gloria had been out there.

Everyone else knew it, too. All the Scrappers

fell silent, and Gloria sat down on the bench and put her glove over her face, as though she couldn't stand to watch anymore.

Still, Ollie knew it wasn't really Cindy's fault. He had thrown a pitch with nothing on it. No wonder the batter had clobbered it. "I'll tell you what you are, Ollie," Ollie said. "You're a big loser. So just throw the ball, lose the game, and get this whole thing over with."

No such luck. Gomez was up, but Ollie couldn't get the ball close enough to get him to swing.

After every pitch, Ollie heard the noise get louder—until everything reached the conclusion the Pit Bulls were waiting for.

Ball four.

Bases loaded.

And then Ollie saw relief. The coach was finally walking to the mound. Ollie could leave the park and go somewhere and hide. He wouldn't have to watch while this great day turned into trash right in front of his eyes.

"I just can't do it," Ollie told the coach.

"Tell me what changed. You were going great there for a while."

"The ump made me stop talking to the ball. Before that, the ball was doing whatever I—"

"Whatever you made it do. Which means, you are some kind of pitcher, young man."

"I can't do it now, though."

Adam had walked to the mound. When Ollie glanced at him, he said, "Sure you can, Ollie. Remember how well you threw when you were over at Gloria's house."

The coach looked down at the grass for a moment. He seemed to be searching for just the right words. "Ollie, all these tricks you use— talking to yourself, talking to the ball—they're just ways to give yourself confidence. When you get scared and worried, you don't throw well. When you think you're going to make a good throw, you do."

Ollie nodded. He knew that was true.

"The only way to have fun—and do your best—is not to worry so much," Coach Carlton said.

"But everybody starts yelling at me—saying I'm crazy and weird and all that stuff. That's what gets to me."

Coach Carlton was about to say something

when Adam said, "Wait. I've got an idea." He turned toward Tracy and yelled, "Talk to your glove, Trace. Tell it to make some great plays."

Tracy looked confused. "What?" she yelled back.

"Go ahead. Start talking to it. That's what we *all* do on this team." Adam turned toward third base. "Talk to your arm, Robbie," he yelled. "Tell it to make a good throw."

Robbie nodded, and then he grinned. He turned toward left field and yelled, "Hey, Trent, talk to your feet. Tell them to be ready to *go* if they have to."

Suddenly, the idea was clear to everyone. Jeremy shouted, "I'm going to talk to my baseball cap. It's my friend."

Wilson stepped out from behind the plate. "I'm talking to my catcher's mitt. I'm going to tell it how much I love it." He whipped off his mitt and gave it a big kiss.

By now the umpire was yelling louder than anyone. "Let's play ball here!"

But all around the diamond, the Scrappers were talking loudly, telling their bodies, their gloves, their shoes, what to do. The Pit Bulls were caught off guard. They weren't saying much of anything. They were just staring out at all the strange things the Scrappers were doing.

The coach looked at Ollie and said, "Well, you're not so weird anymore. You're just like all the rest of the kids on this team." And then he pulled his cap off and said to it, "Hey, be my thinking cap. I don't have much of a brain."

Ollie could hardly believe all this.

"You talk to the ball, or home plate, or anything you want to, Ollie," Adam said. "We're all with you. Every one of us."

Just then Ollie heard Gloria yell, "I talk to my bubble gum. And it talks back to me." She pulled her gum out and held it to her ear. "It says we're going to win this game."

Ollie finally laughed.

CHAPTER TEN

Ollie felt the support. He could hardly believe his teammates would act nuts just to show him they were with him. "If you're weird, so is everyone else," Adam told Ollie. "So do whatever you need to do—but let's get these guys out."

"Okay," Ollie said.

As Adam and the coach walked away, Ollie stepped to the pitching rubber. He took a deep breath and tried to relax. He knew he had to concentrate on the catcher's mitt and forget all the noise—even the noise his teammates were making. He told himself, out loud, "Wilson and I are in a tunnel. We're just playing catch. No one can see us. And here inside, everything is silent."

He got the sign, concentrated on the mitt,

and he whizzed a hard fastball. His motion felt just right.

The batter swung and missed.

So Ollie did it again. The ball was a little inside this time, but the batter took another hard cut—and missed again.

Now Wilson called for the curve, and it was fun for Ollie to watch the pitch break over the plate.

When the umpire's arm shot up, Ollie felt the joy. Now there was one away. But he kept his mind on the catcher's mitt. "Play catch," he told himself again.

Waxman stepped up to the plate. And out there beyond the tunnel, a lot of people were screaming. But Ollie didn't let the noise in.

He got the ball over the plate again, and Waxman took a huge cut. He got only a piece of the ball, and it dribbled onto the grass and rolled straight toward Ollie.

Wilson jumped in front of the plate and shouted, "Home! Home!"

Ollie grabbed the ball and made a quick underhanded toss back to Wilson for a force-out at the plate.

Wayment, of all people, was coming up to bat. Suddenly Ollie realized that he could still win this game. All he had to do was get one more out. With that thought, all the noise came thundering back into his ears. The tunnel seemed to disappear.

"Don't swing!" someone yelled. "Ollie will walk you."

"No!" Ollie told himself. "Don't listen to that." But he felt the worry coming back.

Then he heard Adam. "You can do it, Ollie. You can get him."

He looked over and saw Adam pump his fist. Ollie nodded back to him. At the same time he heard all his other teammates yelling the same kind of stuff. No one was acting funny now; they were just telling him they believed in him.

Ollie stepped off the mound and looked at the mountains and the sky. The afternoon sun was angling lower, the blue of the sky deepening. He looked into that blue, and he took another deep breath. "No tricks," he told himself. "You can pitch. Just do it."

He knew the right motion. All he needed to do was feel it, do it, and forget *everything* else. He returned to the pitching rubber, took his signal, saw that mitt, and started into his motion.

And it felt right.

He released the ball with a good wrist snap, followed through, and the pitch was right where he wanted it. At the knees and hard.

But Wayment crunched it.

The ball took off like a cannon shot, heading for the fence in right center.

Ollie felt all the air go out of him.

Jeremy was running hard, trying to get to it, but Ollie knew he didn't have a chance. Even if the ball stayed in the park, it was over Jeremy's head.

And then Ollie saw Thurlow streaking from right field. He was jetting along on a line that was going to take him into the fence.

Ollie cringed, but Thurlow closed on the ball, pulled up just in time, and then jumped high in the air, with his arm stretched out.

For a moment, Ollie couldn't tell what had happened. And then Thurlow turned toward the infield and held his glove in the air. Something white—like a scoop of vanilla on top of an ice-cream cone—was showing above the fingers of his glove.

"*Out!*" the umpire bellowed.

Ollie still couldn't believe it. He had had all that time—those seconds while the ball was in the air—to get used to the idea that Wayment had hit a grand slam. He could hardly get his head back to thinking the game was over and the Scrappers had won.

But then he saw Adam running at him. "You did it, Ollie. You did it," he was hollering.

"Thurlow did it!" Ollie told him.

"The whole team did it!"

All the players crowded around Ollie, and everyone gave him a pat on the back. "Thanks, you guys," Ollie kept yelling to them.

Coach Carlton finally had a chance to put his arm around Ollie's shoulder. "Nice job," he said. "We've got us a pitcher we can depend on now. You pitch like that, and you're going to be tough to hit all season."

"Coach, I *lost* that game. Thurlow just ran out there and stole it back."

"Just a minute. I want to talk to you about that." The coach raised his voice and said, "Kids, I want you all to shake hands with the Pit Bull players and then meet over by the dugout. I have a few things I want to say to you."

The players lined up for the traditional hand-slapping. Then Ollie had a chance to talk to his mom and dad for a minute.

"We're proud of you," his mother said, and she hugged him. She and his dad had on dark glasses and shorts. Ollie had to laugh because they both thought they were so cool.

"I have the feeling you got some things straight in your head today," his father said. He hugged Ollie, too.

"Well, you know *my* head. Nothing's ever too straight in there," Ollie said.

"Hey, thank goodness for that," his mom said. "We like *interesting* people around our house."

"And interesting dogs," Ollie told her.

"Winnie's doing a little better, you know," his mom said, and she laughed. "You just have to have faith in her, the way I do."

"I think I will from now on."

By then the coach was calling for the kids—and families—to come over. He waited until they gathered, and then he said, "I just want to say a couple of things. Maybe give you something to think about.

"First off, I want you kids to remember what happened when you all started pulling for each other. It's not just something coaches say. When players back each other up, everything changes. I think you felt some of that. It can only get better, if we keep it up."

Ollie looked around for Thurlow. He was standing, not sitting with the other kids, but at least he had stuck around. Ollie knew he was one player who had to be more a part of the team if the Scrappers were going to have any chance for the second-half championship.

"There's something else you need to keep straight," Mr. Carlton said. "Ollie told me that Thurlow won the game for you kids just now."

That brought a cheer from all the players.

"No, no. Wait a minute. You've got to think about this right. Ollie threw a very good pitch. He did his part. The batter hit the ball anyway, and that's when Thurlow did his part. But all of you were doing something—heading to the right spot to cover a base or to back someone up. See, that's baseball. You got that batter out together—*all* of you. And you won this game together. That's how it always is, win or lose."

"Thurlow just said the right things to his glove—and to his feet," Jeremy said, and he laughed.

The coach smiled, but then he said, "Adam had a good idea when he got you kids doing that stuff. And you know why it worked? Ollie found out you were on his side—not back there doubting him. That's how everyone on the team needs to feel."

"That's right," Ollie mumbled, and then he caught himself. Sooner or later, he would have to *think* the right thoughts without saying everything out loud.

"All right. We practice on Monday, and play again on Tuesday. Remember, in one way, this game didn't mean a thing. The Mustangs won the first-half championship, and we ended up fourth or fifth, depending on what the Whirlwinds do today. But we can win the second half and still win the championship for the season— if we play the way we did at times today."

Now there was a bigger cheer, with all the parents joining in.

"I also expect you to attend an important meeting that Mr. Lubak has called." Coach

Carlton hesitated, and then he smiled. "He says that if you'll all walk across the street to Granny's, he's buying the ice cream. Attendance is not mandatory, but it's highly recommended."

One more cheer went up.

As everyone stood up, Ollie spotted Thurlow moving away and ran after him. "Come on, Thurlow, go with us. You deserve a banana split or a big—"

"Naw. I don't want to."

"Why not?"

Thurlow shrugged, and then he said, "I don't know."

"Come with us then."

Thurlow shrugged again, and some seconds passed. Then he said, "All right."

Ollie knew that was a breakthrough.

At Granny's, everyone seemed to have plenty to talk about. They were remembering the big plays, the big hits, and they were vowing to win the second-half championship. But it wasn't just talk anymore. Ollie could tell that the players really believed they could do it.

TIPS FOR PITCHING

1. Control is the key to good pitching. Speed won't help you if your pitches aren't over the plate. Practice until you can throw the ball in the strike zone. Once you have that mastered, learn to move the ball up and down, in and out.
2. Rely on your fastball. Your coach can help you decide when to start trying curves and sliders. If you start too young, you can hurt your arm. As a beginner, a fastball in a good spot is your best pitch.
3. Grip the ball with your thumb on the bottom and your index and middle fingers on top. Keep a little space between the ball and the palm of your hand. Your wrist should snap as you release the ball. Some pitchers grip across the seams, others, with the seams. Experiment to see what works best for you.
4. Use the same motion on every pitch. Work with your coach to develop a strong, smooth motion, and then practice until your muscles know how to repeat it.
5. Throw the ball; don't aim it. With a good grip and a good motion—and your eye on the target—release the ball to the catcher's glove. If you "point" the ball or try to "push" it to the right place, you lose both speed and accuracy.
6. Once you've mastered your fastball, you may

want to learn a change-up to keep batters off balance. Grip the ball against the palm of your hand and throw it as though you were throwing a fastball. It will look like a fastball when you release it but will get to the plate much slower.

7. The moment you pitch the ball, you become an infielder. If the ball is hit past you to the right side of the infield, run to first base in case you need to cover for the first baseman, who might have to field the ball. Run toward the first base line, then turn and run parallel to it. This puts you in a good position to take the throw.

8. Backing up the bases is essential. Cover home on a throw from the outfield. When that kind of play is developing, run to a point behind the plate (maybe ten feet or so), and be ready to stop the ball if it gets past the catcher. Always back up third base on a throw from the outfield. If a runner is on third base, it's your responsibility to cover the plate if a pitch gets past the catcher.

9. Learn to keep runners close to their bases. Most leagues for younger players don't allow stealing. As you get older, however, you will have to develop a "move" to the bases. A quick, accurate throw is more important than a fast one. Practice your move to each base. When the catcher attempts to throw out a runner at second base, duck or move off the mound to avoid being hit with the ball, but don't turn your back to the plate.

10. Don't overwork your arm when you're young. Most leagues have rules about the number of innings a young player can pitch in one week. If your league doesn't, be careful. Practice, but don't throw so hard and so often that you hurt your arm.

SOME RULES FROM COACH CARLTON

HITTING:

As you swing, stride forward. Start with your weight slightly back, then move toward the ball as it travels to the plate. Don't step toward the plate or away from it (that's called "stepping in the bucket"); stride parallel to the plate, toward the mound.

BASE RUNNING:

When you run to first base after you've hit the ball to the infield, run on a straight line and overrun the base. Don't slow down until you're past the base.

BEING A TEAM PLAYER:

Learn from your coach. Listen and cooperate during practice sessions. Play as hard during practice as you do during a game. You'll improve much faster and inspire others to do the same.

The Whirlwinds hadn't played well, but they weren't about to give up. The first batter let a couple of bad pitches go by, then hit a hard-shot grounder past Tracy for a single. Thurlow tossed the ball in to Tracy, who relayed it back to Adam.

Adam did show some effort with the next batter. He tried to put some more "umph" behind his throws. The trouble was, he was missing. He walked the batter on a 3 and 1 pitch that looked like a perfect strike to Gloria.

"Come on, ump," she yelled, but then she stopped herself.

"Come on, kids, let's talk it up out there," Coach Carlton yelled. "We can't let these guys get back in this game!"

At least he sounded concerned.

The players did start some chatter. Gloria even yelled, "All right. Take two if you can, but get the sure one." No one could misunderstand something like that.

Bailey, the ninth batter, was coming to the plate. The Scrappers still didn't have an out. They needed this one before the top of the order went to work. But the umpire called a couple of pretty good pitches balls, and suddenly Adam was only two pitches from filling the bases. The next one was coming down the middle, and everyone knew it, including the batter.

Bailey didn't have much power, but he took a fluid stroke and poked a grounder to the left side. Gloria broke to her right, stretched, and backhanded the ball. She thought she might have a chance for the double play. She stopped, set her feet, and took a quick look to second. But she decided in an instant that she better take the sure out at third.

She spun and tossed a quick little throw to Robbie. But he wasn't ready. He was at the bag, but he was looking toward second. He reacted quickly, got his glove up, but Gloria had thrown awfully hard, considering how close she was. The ball bounced off Robbie's glove, then his chest, and dropped onto the grass. He dived after it, grabbed it, and tried to tag the runner, but he was too late.

"Come on, Robbie!" Gloria shouted. "Be alive. What were you thinking?"

Robbie jumped up. He looked angry. "You looked at second. I thought you were going that way."

"Didn't you hear what I just told everybody? Take two if you can, but get the sure one. I had to take a look, but—"

"Gloria, never mind," the coach said. He was walking toward her. He put his hand on her shoulder and said, quietly, "You had time to look back at Robbie and give him time to get set. You hurried your throw more than you needed to."

"No way, Coach. My throw was on the money. He was gawking off in space somewhere."

"Gloria. Come on."

Oh, brother. It was time for another speech. But Gloria wasn't going to hear it. She twisted away from him and walked back to her position.

The whole team was silent now. All the chatter had stopped. Then Jeremy yelled, "Shake it off, Gloria. Don't worry about it. Let's get this next guy."

Gloria turned and looked at Jeremy. She felt like running out to center field and pounding on that little shrimp. Hadn't he seen the play? It was Robbie who had messed up. But she only gave Jeremy a long glare, and then she turned back to see whether Adam could throw a decent pitch.

"I'm surrounded by losers," she mumbled to herself.

As Chuck Kenny stepped to the plate, the Whirlwinds really started whooping it up in the dugout. It was time for Adam to reach back and find some reserve strength. Either that, or they ought to try someone else—like Thurlow. If the coach would give the guy a chance, he could be a great pitcher.

But Adam decided it was time to get cute. Instead of throwing his hard stuff, he tried a change-up. Chuck almost jumped out of his shoes, the pitch looked so big. He got around on it and *thrashed* it. It was a spear, and it was flashing past Robbie when he lunged to his left and got a glove on it. It glanced sideways off the tip of his glove, straight toward Gloria.

The carom caught Gloria off guard, but she was able to reach down and scoop up the ball. She was off balance, but she recovered and fired the ball to second base. Tracy was ready. The ball no sooner hit her glove than she spun and whipped it to first.

The play at first was close. Gloria actually thought the runner beat the ball, but the umpire jerked his arm in the air. "Yerout!"

The Whirlwinds couldn't believe it. Their coach ran across the diamond, straight at the umpire. He was screaming, "That boy wasn't out. What are you talking about?"

But the umpire walked away from him and didn't reply.

Gloria loved it. One run had scored, but the Scrappers still had a big lead, 11 to 5. She laughed and yelled, "Two down. Take the easy one."

But she saw Ollie hurry to the mound and begin talking to Adam. She wondered what that was about, so she trotted over. When she got there, Ollie said, "That guy was safe. I know he was. Do you think we should tell the umpire?"

Gloria stared at Ollie for several seconds before she finally said, "Are you brain-dead? Are you on life support? Do I see tubes running up your nose?"

Adam said, "Lay off, Gloria. He just didn't know what you're supposed to do."

"Umpires call the plays, you pea brain. He wouldn't change his call just because *you* think the guy was safe—no more than he did for the Whirlwinds' coach."

Ollie looked as though he had been hit in the head with a bat. He mumbled, "I just thought . . . ," and then he turned and walked away.

"Is this a zoo?" Gloria asked. She looked around. "Who let all the cuckoo birds out to play?"

"Lay off," Adam said.

"Let's see you make me."

"Gloria!" The coach was jogging to the mound. "Calm down. What's the matter?"

"I've tried all day to keep my mouth shut, but I can't do it. These people don't even know the game. They have black holes where their brains are supposed to be."

Adam looked at the coach, who appeared confused. "Ollie thought that guy was safe. He wondered if he should tell the umpire."

Ollie was walking back toward the mound by then. "That's all right," the coach told him. "We let the umpires make the calls."

Ollie nodded.

Gloria was still dumbfounded.

"Do you see why I can't keep my mouth shut?"

"No, Gloria, I don't," the coach said. "But I'll tell you this much. You're about to leave this game again, and this time, you can just keep walking. I've tried all summer to get you to stop yelling at people, and nothing works."

Gloria rolled her eyes, and then she took a long breath. She began counting to ten as she turned to walk away. But just at that moment, Adam said, "I'd kick her off the team, Coach. She thinks she knows everything. She gets everybody messed up."

That was more than Gloria could handle. She spun around and yelled, "Adam, if you could pitch—even just a little—I wouldn't have to yell at you."

"Shut up, Gloria," Adam said. "Or come over here and say that."

Gloria knew she couldn't let that go by. She ran straight at him. Adam stood his ground, seeming unsure what she had in mind. But Gloria never stopped. She drove her shoulder straight into Adam's gut.

Adam folded like a jackknife and went down hard.

Gloria jumped up and stood over him. "Get

up and fight me," she said. "Come on. Let's go."

But Adam curled up on his side. He was holding his stomach and moaning.

Ollie stepped toward the mound. "Do you want a piece of me, too?" Gloria yelled. "Go ahead. Take the first swing."

Ollie was stunned. "Swing?" he said. "Are you crazy?" He knelt down next to Adam.

But Gloria realized too late that he was only checking on Adam. She slammed him in the side of the head with her glove. He fell over and then scrambled up to his feet. "What's wrong with you?" he said.

But now everyone was coming over. Tracy tried to grab Gloria, but Gloria spun away, only to be grabbed by Thurlow, who seemed to have appeared out of nowhere. "Let me go," she shouted, but he had his arms around her, from behind, and he was holding her tight.

By now the Whirlwinds had crowded around, too. And the umpires were there. Gloria was still fighting to get loose, and she saw everything in a blur.

"You're out of this game," the home plate umpire told Gloria.

Like that was big news.

And then Coach Carlton spoke in a calm voice. "This game is over," he said. "We forfeit."

"No, Coach," Wilson yelled. "We've got the game won."

"That doesn't matter one bit to me," Coach Carlton said.

"Just kick Gloria off the team," Adam said. He was getting up now.

"What team?" the coach said. "Without a coach, you don't have a team. And I'm not going to coach you kids anymore. So you better start looking for a new coach."

Suddenly, the focus changed. All the Scrappers moved toward Coach Carlton. Gloria felt Thurlow's arms loosen, and she jerked away from him.

"Don't do this, Coach," Adam was pleading. "We want to play."

"No, you don't," the coach said. "You want to have fistfights. I know baseball, and this isn't it. I don't want anything more to do with this bunch."

And he headed for the parking lot.